THE BUFFALO'S LAST STAND

Crossway Books Youth Series by Stephen Bly

THE NATHAN T. RIGGINS WESTERN ADVENTURE SERIES
The Dog Who Would Not Smile
Coyote True
You Can Always Trust a Spotted Horse
The Last Stubborn Buffalo in Nevada
Never Dance with a Bobcat
Hawks Don't Say Good-bye

THE LEWIS AND CLARK SQUAD ADVENTURE SERIES
Intrigue at the Rafter B Ranch
The Secret of the Old Rifle
Treachery at the River Canyon
Revenge on Eagle Island
Danger at Deception Pass
Hazards of the Half-Court Press

RETTA BARRE'S OREGON TRAIL SERIES
The Lost Wagon Train
The Buffalo's Last Stand
The Plain Prairie Princess

~ Retta Barre's Oregon Trail ~

BOOK TWO

THE BUFFALO'S LAST STAND

⚜ STEPHEN BLY ⚜

CROSSWAY BOOKS

A DIVISION OF
GOOD NEWS PUBLISHERS
WHEATON, ILLINOIS

The Buffalo's Last Stand

Copyright © 2002 by Stephen Bly

Published by Crossway Books

          a division of Good News Publishers

          1300 Crescent Street

          Wheaton, Illinois 60187

Cover design: David LaPlaca

Cover illustrator: Bill Dodge

First printing 2002

Printed in the United States of America

Library of Congress Cataloging-in-Publication Data

Bly, Stephen A., 1944 -

   The buffalo's last stand / Stephen Bly.

      p.   cm. — (Retta Barre's Oregon Trail ; Book 2)

   Summary: On the Oregon Trail in 1852, twelve-year-old Retta helps negotiate with a renegade Arapaho when he captures her new Shoshone friend, Shy Bear, and a girl from the wagon train. Then she faces a wounded buffalo.

   ISBN 1-58134-392-2 (TPB : alk. paper)

   1. Oregon National Historic Trail—Juvenile fiction. [1. Oregon National Historic Trail—Fiction. 2. Frontier and pioneer life—West (U.S.)— Fiction. 3. Indians of North America—Fiction. 4. West (U.S.)—Fiction.] I. Title. II. Series.

PZ7.B6275 Bu   2002

[Fic]—dc21   2001007098

                                                 CIP

15	14	13	12	11	10	09	08	07	06	05	04	03	02
15	14	13	12	11	10	9	8	7	6	5	4	3	2	1

For
Natalia Puebla

*Who knows
whether you have not come to the kingdom
for such a time as this?*

ESTHER 4:14 ESV

One

Along the North Platte River, two days west of Robidoux's Trading Post, near Scotts Bluff, Tuesday, June 29, 1852

> *Dear Diary,*
> *I think he likes me. I could tell it by the way he ran away. Boys are like that, Joslyn says. And Joslyn knows. If nothing else exciting ever happens in my life, perhaps this day has been enough.*
>
> *Coretta Emily Barre, 12½*

Retta jammed her journal into the back of the covered wagon. She licked her fingers and tried to mash her thick dark brown bangs flat against her forehead. Then she plopped down on an upturned bucket under the canvas awning attached to their wagon so she could scrape mud off her shoes. The air felt warm, with the shouts of men and the painful shrieks of wagon wheels drifting on a slight breeze. Retta's mother climbed down out of the wagon with slow, deliberate steps.

Mrs. Barre paused by Retta and fastened the tiny buttons on her cuffs. "You're a muddy mess, young lady. What have you been doing?"

Retta brushed a fly off her cheek, leaving another streak

of mud. "William told us to stay out of the way while they moved the California wagons to the front. So some of us hiked over to the river—that's all."

Mrs. Barre licked her fingers and smoothed down the back of Retta's hair. "Is it dry enough to move wagons?" she asked.

"I don't think so 'cause they surely are making a mess." Retta stood and gently hugged her mother's waist. "How are you feeling now, Mama?"

Mrs. Barre slipped her arm around Retta's shoulder. "Better, thank you, baby. I needed that nap. I don't like feeling so tired all the time. Did you get your moccasins?"

Retta held up the knee-high deerskin moccasins. "Look, Mama, aren't they pretty? They are a little worn where they have been rubbing against a horse, but that won't matter, especially when I get my very own pinto."

"What is this talk about a pinto?"

"Mama, I want to buy a horse for this journey."

"You know what I said about ladies riding horses."

"But, Mama, I don't have to be a lady until I get to Oregon, do I? Ladies stay in the wagon and sew. Girls go out and pick up buffalo chips."

Mrs. Barre allowed a small smile. "That's an interesting definition. Perhaps it does add weight to your cause."

"I only have a few dollars saved, and there's no chestnut and white pinto around anyway. So I guess it's no more than a little girl's dream."

"You aren't all that little."

"Lerryn says I am."

"Yes, well, compared to big sis, I suppose you are a little girl."

"Compared to her, I look like a boy!"

"Coretta!"

"How do you like my moccasins, Mama?" Retta held them up again.

"They're beautiful. I don't think that little book was worth this much."

"Two Bears was very happy with the trade."

"I must say I'm impressed. Anyone who wants to read *Pilgrim's Progress* is a wise man. I wonder if he's seen the light?"

"You mean, become a Christian?"

"Yes. I heard that some Indians are coming to Jesus. There are missionaries, you know. But poor Dr. and Mrs. Whitman . . . poor, poor lady." Mrs. Barre rubbed her forehead.

"Two Bears said he wanted to find the path to heaven." Retta saw a tear trickle out of her mother's eye. "Mama, did you see my note? I left you a note before I went to the river."

"Yes. You need to practice your penmanship, young lady. I can hardly tell your *v* from your *n*." Mrs. Barre peered into a pail in which small white beans were soaking.

"I write in my journal every day."

"That's nice, baby."

"I actually had something to say today. Imagine meeting Indians face to face."

"Let's make that the last trip to meet Indians without your brothers or your father along. Not all Indians are friendly. Now wash your cheek."

Retta found a small flour sack towel and wiped her whole face. "Joslyn, Christen, and Ben went with me."

Mrs. Barre plucked out a white bean from the pail and chewed on it. "That's good. I'm glad young Ben went along to look after you girls."

Retta bit her lip and puffed out her cheeks. *Ben Weaver was about as much help as a log chained to my ankle.*

Mrs. Barre waved her out from under the awning. "Now hurry and find your papa. Ask him if we are rotating our wagon or if I should fix supper here. I can't imagine moving wagons in this mud. And send Lerryn this way if you spot her. She was getting some help with her memory quilt from Mrs. Ferdinand."

As Retta hiked past the wagons, seven-year-old Taggie Potts caught up with her. "Taggie, how come you have a string on Santana?" she asked.

The boy tugged on his ripped hat and looked down at his skinny black dog. "Ain't a string. It's a leash."

Retta leaned over and petted the head of the smiling dog. "You have to leash him?"

Taggie's brown eyes widened. "Yep. Don't you know that there're Injuns around? I'm afraid they might eat him!"

Retta stared at the ribs on the small dog. *Someone would have to be dying of starvation to even think of eating that dog.*

Taggie rubbed dirty fingers across the beaded sleeve of her buckskin dress. "Did you really see the Injuns, Retta?"

"Yes, I did, Taggie. I met some very nice Indians."

"Did you talk Indian to them?"

"One of them knew English. But there was another one who didn't. He was a bit scary."

Taggie reached up and put his sticky hand in hers as they hiked around the Swanson wagon. "Did he have any scalps on his belt?"

"No."

"Did he have a bow and arrow?"

"No."

"Did he have a rifle?"

"No, but he did have a hunting knife."

Taggie's eyes widened. "Ansley said that Injuns have

rings in their noses. Did this one have a ring in his nose, Retta?"

"No, but he did have some scars on his cheeks," Retta said. "I wonder why Ansley said that? She didn't go with us to see the Indians."

"She didn't?"

"No."

"Are you scared of Injuns, Retta? I ain't scared of them." He clutched her hand more tightly. "Well, maybe just a little."

Retta could feel the soles of her shoes sink into the dirt, but the mud no longer stuck to her heels. "Taggie, did you see those six men who camped with us at the river crossing last week?"

"The ones who smelled funny and had big guns strapped to their belts?"

"The very ones. Did they scare you?"

"Yeah."

"Were they Indians?" she pressed.

"Nope."

"Well, they scared me, too. So I reckon there are some scary people all over. Some are Indian, and some are white."

"Yeah, sometimes I'm scared of my papa," Taggie admitted.

Retta put her hand on Taggie's shoulder as they walked up the line of wagons. *When your daddy takes to whiskey, all of us are scared.*

She stopped to stare at the open space where Joslyn's wagon had recently been. There were foot-deep muddy ruts leading away from the spot.

"The California-bound folks done pulled out," Taggie announced.

She stared toward the head of the line of wagons.

"They put them up front this evening, but they aren't actually leaving until first thing in the morning."

Taggie squatted down and petted his dog. "No, they all pulled out for them hills up there. I seen 'em and waved good-bye."

Retta squatted down next to Taggie and scratched her head. "What do you mean, they left? The Landers surely didn't leave. Joslyn was with me for the last couple of hours."

"Your brother gave her a ride up to them. They left, I tell you. It was really muddy. You should have seen it."

Retta shaded her eyes against the setting sun. "They can't just leave like that. No one leaves in the evening." She sprinted toward the front of the mile-long wagon train.

"I'm goin' to stay here," Taggie shouted. "Santana don't want to run."

Retta slowed near a tall Conestoga with red-spoked wheels and a blue box. She saw Mrs. Ferdinand rummaging in a valise on a rocking chair beside the wagon.

"Retta, I have something for you to take to your sister."

"Oh, Mrs. Ferdinand . . . hi!" Retta gasped for breath. "Isn't Lerryn here with you?"

"Oh, no. She only stopped by for a minute, but I promised to find her this star pattern. Would you see that she gets it?"

Retta grabbed the neatly folded large paper star. "Do you know where she went?"

"I believe she said she had to help Joslyn pack. They're going to California, you know."

Retta hustled up to the lead wagon just as her brother Andrew rode up on Beanie.

"Where are the California wagons?" she called out.

"Just over that next rise, wallowing in the mud and making a mess of the prairie."

"Did you take Joslyn up there?"

"Do you mean River Raven? She insisted that I call her that." His light brown hair curled out from under his floppy-brimmed gray felt hat.

Retta stepped up and rubbed Beanie's dun-colored neck. "River Raven is her Indian name."

"Did you go see your Indian?"

"Yes, but why does everyone keep calling Two Bears *my* Indian?" Retta stood in front of the horse and leaned her open eye close to Beanie's.

Andrew reined the horse back. "'Cause you're the only one who has seen him."

"Not anymore." Retta watched the sun drop behind the distant horizon. "I can't believe she's gone just like that," she murmured. "It makes me sick to my stomach that I didn't get to say good-bye."

"Her stepdaddy went off without her. Said she could walk and catch up, and that he wasn't waitin'. That seemed wrong to me; so I figured the least I could do was give her a ride up to the wagon."

Retta folded her arms across her chest. "But I didn't get to tell her good-bye properly."

"I did," Andrew grinned.

Retta spun around and grabbed his stirrup. "What did you mean by that?"

His wide smile revealed twin dimples. "She hugged me and gave me a kiss right on the cheek."

"She did not," Retta fumed.

"Yes, she did."

"But—but you're my brother! She can't kiss my brother."

"I'm not her brother."

Retta puffed out her cheeks and sputtered, "You can't go around kissing my friends!"

"I didn't." He winked. "She kissed me."

Retta waited by the flap of the dingy white tent. Three men huddled inside around a small folding table covered with maps. She jumped when she heard her father's voice. "You lookin' for me, darlin'?"

Retta stuck her head into the tent and asked, "Sorry to bother you, Papa. Mama wants to know if she should cook supper where we are, or are we rotating the wagons first?"

Mr. Barre glanced at Colonel Graves hovering over a map. "I don't reckon it's worth movin' this late in the day," the colonel said.

Bobcat Bouchet scratched his shaggy gray beard. "No danger from Missy's Indian, I reckon. Shoshones are a fairly peaceful lot. Course, he's a long way from home. That makes 'em more peaceful sometimes."

"I'm sure you don't have to worry about Two Bears. I gave him a copy of *Pilgrim's Progress*."

"Is he in camp?" the colonel asked.

"No, some of us went out to his place," Retta replied.

Bobcat Bouchet rubbed his beard. "You found him?"

She dropped her chin to her chest. "He sort of found us."

"Next time how about takin' me along?" Bobcat suggested. "I want to know what he knows about this country. I assume he's been through it before."

"He's going to Fort Bridger."

"He is?" Bobcat pulled off his felt hat and rubbed his dirty forehead on his dirty shirtsleeve. "He's got a few hundred miles left."

Retta rocked back on her heels. "I think that's his home. The government wanted him down in the Indian Territory, but he doesn't have any family there. So he left. It's not easy for the Shoshone to get along with the Cherokee. I think it's silly to stick them all in the same place."

The colonel gave Mr. Barre a sharp look. "Eugene, did it dawn on you that this young lady knows more about the Indians in the area than any of us?"

Retta held her breath and puffed out her cheeks.

Mr. Barre studied his daughter's face. "I've got a feelin' she has a little more to say. What else do you know, darlin'?"

"I saw an Arapaho Indian named Tall Owl," she blurted out.

"Arapaho!" Bobcat Bouchet leaped to his feet and grabbed his rifle.

"Already? I was hoping we wouldn't see them for two more weeks." The colonel chewed on the stem of his unlit clay pipe and tapped his foot as if listening to a march.

"Did he look friendly?" Bouchet asked.

"No, sir. He looked mean," Retta reported.

Colonel Graves waved his hand. "Eugene, we need to organize the wagons. Put them in two parallel lines fifty feet apart, even if we have to double up on the oxen to pull them through the mud. You get your boys and bring the horses and cattle into the middle."

Then he turned to the grizzled scout. "Bobcat, take two men with you and ride up to that California-bound bunch and tell them the Arapaho are nearby. Tell them to post extra guards and reconsider if they really want to split off." The colonel's arms waved as he punched out the orders. "It would be safer if they stuck with us at least until South Pass . . . but we've been down that line of thinkin' with them before."

"It's really that serious?" Mr. Barre asked.

Bobcat nodded. "The picnic's over. Now comes the hard work. I never thought Tall Owl would come this far north and west. We're in Cheyenne and Sioux country."

"You know him?" Retta asked.

"Never met him face to face. Did you actually see him up close?"

Retta stepped inside the tent. "Yes, but Two Bears and his sons chased him off."

Bobcat held his rifle in his right hand and rubbed his beard with his left. "Arapahos chased by a Shoshone family?"

Retta bit her lip and rocked back on her heels. "Only one Arapaho. Tall Owl was by himself."

Bobcat Bouchet paced the tent. "Why was he alone?"

"Maybe he was scouting," Mr. Barre suggested.

"He usually has a whole band with him," Colonel Graves said.

"He's in trouble," Bobcat mumbled. "Maybe they kicked him out again. Was he carryin' a weapon?"

"A huge knife," Retta reported.

"No bow and arrow?"

"Nope."

"No gun?"

"Nope."

Colonel Graves moved closer to Retta. "Did you happen to notice if his horse was tired?"

"I didn't see a horse. I think he was on foot. He just ran off into the brush."

"That don't make sense," Bobcat muttered as though to himself. "Unless his band was just around the corner."

"Bring the livestock in. We've got to get these wagons moved up right away," the colonel shouted as he barged out of the tent.

Retta crept over and slipped her hand into her father's. "Papa, is Colonel Graves mad at me?"

"No, darlin'. He thinks you're tellin' the truth, and he respects your word."

"I am telling the truth," she replied.

"I know, baby. Now run back and tell Mama to pack

the outfit. We are movin' the wagon after all. But don't tell her we're expectin' Indians to attack. This is just a safety measure. There's no reason for her to worry. Your mama has enough worries without us addin' more."

Retta sprinted back down the line of wagons.

Taggie trotted up. "Are the Indians really goin' to attack?" he hollered.

"Where did you hear that?" she challenged.

"I sort of listened in from outside the tent."

"You can't tell anyone. It might not be as bad as they think."

"I didn't tell no one . . . except Travis Lott . . . and maybe Johnny Dillard."

When Retta reached the big Conestoga, Mrs. Ferdinand was tossing pots and pans into the back. "Get to your wagon, Retta darlin'. There are Indians at the top of the rise, and they'll attack any minute now!"

Two

Bobcat Bouchet rode back into camp right after dark along two parallel lines of wagons parked in the mud. Cattle and horses milled around between the rigs. Colonel Graves's wagon served as the front gate, and old Sven Neilsen's heavy freight wagon was the back gate.

Lerryn washed dishes near the tailgate of the Barre wagon. Retta hovered next to her, cotton tea towel in hand.

"Mother, can you hear me?" Lerryn called out.

"Yes, I'm just resting a moment. Are you through with the dishes?"

"No, but I was wondering if I could ride in Mrs. Ferdinand's wagon tomorrow. I'm learning so much about quilting."

"That will be fine. Only don't wander away from the wagon train—not with Indians about. Coretta Emily can help me if I need anything."

"What if I wanted to walk with Christen? Would you stay with Mama?" Retta whispered to her sister.

Lerryn kept her voice low. "I have more important things to do than just play with my friends."

"I suspect you won't be thinking about quilts tomorrow," Retta challenged.

"And just what do you mean by that?"

"I went by Mrs. Ferdinand's. You weren't there. She said you had only stopped by for a minute."

"That's nonsense. Mrs. Ferdinand is forgetful. We worked on a star pattern."

"She said she couldn't find her star pattern. That's why she gave it to me to bring to you."

"You have my pattern?"

"It's up in the wagon on your mattress."

"Why were you spying on me?"

"Mother sent me to fetch you," Retta retorted.

"She did not," Lerryn snapped.

"Ask her."

"What are you saying?"

"I think you lied to Mama so you could be with Brian Suetter."

Lerryn slammed a cast-iron skillet into the wash pan. A wave of suds splashed toward Retta. "You'll understand someday."

The two girls finished doing dishes in silence. Then Retta's voice softened. "What's it like, Lerryn?" she whispered.

"What is what like?"

Retta let her chin drop to her chest. "You know . . . kissing a boy . . . and stuff."

Lerryn brushed her bangs off her forehead and stared out into the dark prairie sky. A smile broke across her face. "It's sweet."

"It is?"

Lerryn stuck her hands back into the water. "Yes, especially if you warm him up first."

Retta draped the dishtowel over her head like a scarf and peeked out. "Do what?"

"Hold his hand a little."

Retta chewed on a corner of the towel. "Papa says boys

act like stupid dolts around girls. Does Brian act like a stupid dolt?"

"He most certainly does not. That's the kind of thing papas say to their daughters to keep them at home until they're twenty."

"How does it feel to know that a boy really, really, really likes you?" Retta quizzed.

"You've never had a boy who really, really, really likes you?"

Retta dried off an enameled tin pie plate. "Nope."

"How about Ben?"

"Sometimes he sort of likes me. But he really, really, really likes Ansley."

"Does that bother you?"

"Nope. Well, sort of. I just don't like the way Ansley always shows off and pretends to be so much better than me. Yeah, I guess it does bother me."

"There are always people like that." Lerryn scrubbed a knife long after it was clean.

"People don't treat you that way, do they?"

"Maybe not exactly the same, but there's always someone you're competing with, I guess."

"Who do you have to compete with, Lerryn? I overheard one of William's friends say you are the cutest girl in the wagon train."

Lerryn threw her shoulders back. "Who said that?"

"The one they call Cherokee Washington."

"He said I'm the cutest?"

"He said that William's sister is the cutest girl on the wagon train. He certainly didn't mean me. So who do you have to compete with?"

"The queen," Lerryn whispered.

"What do you mean, the queen? There's no queen on the wagon train."

"Yes, there is."

"Who? I don't know any queen. Is she in disguise?"

"No." Lerryn splashed another pan into the dirty dish-water. "Who does Papa call the queen?"

Retta's face brightened. "Mama? You have to compete with Mama?"

Lerryn took a big, deep breath and held it.

"Really, Lerryn?"

"You don't know how lucky you are, Retta."

"What do you mean?"

"Which of us looks like Mama?"

"You do. I don't look like anybody in our family."

"Precisely. So everyone compares me to Mama. I have to live up to her standards."

"But Mama is old."

"Thirty-eight is not that old. And it's not just her looks. Everyone thinks I should be as smart and wise and kind and talented as Mama. Sometimes they even call me Julia by mistake."

"They do?"

"Did anyone ever call you Julia?"

"No!" Retta giggled.

"Did they ever call you Eugene?"

Retta laughed. "No, of course not."

"You see. You get to grow up being Coretta Emily Barre. That's all you have to be. Totally yourself. But I have to grow up being Julia Carter Barre, Jr."

For several minutes, neither sister spoke. Finally Lerryn dried her hands on Retta's damp cotton towel. She brushed her blonde hair back off her forehead and stared up the line of wagons. "It's sweet," she whispered. "Real sweet."

"The kisses?"

"Yes."

"What about the other stuff?"

The sound of someone running in the dark caused both girls to peek around the wagon.

"Retta!" a voice called out.

"It's William," Lerryn said.

Retta grabbed her sister's arm. "What about the stuff?"

"I'll tell you later," Lerryn promised.

"When?"

"In about three years."

"Retta! Papa needs you," William shouted.

"Where is he?" she asked.

"Up with the colonel."

"He needs me?"

"You're our Indian expert."

"That's a laugh."

"Come on, they're waitin' for you," William insisted.

"For me? Really?"

"You see, Coretta Emily, you get to be you!" Lerryn maintained.

Retta hurried to keep up with her brother's long strides.

"What did Lerryn mean by that?" he asked.

"Oh, it's just . . ."

"Girl chat?"

"Yes." *I don't think Lerryn and I ever had a "girl chat" in our lives. Maybe this was the first.* "William, slow down. It's dark and I can't keep up."

"Here, take my hand." He slipped his fingers in hers. Her brother's hand was warm, callused, and strong.

Retta scurried almost at a trot. *I bet Ben Weaver's hand is not strong like William's. Lord, I really like my brothers. And I guess I like Lerryn a lot more than I thought I did. How come I always think everyone else has it easier than me? Except Ansley . . . she really does have it easy.*

When they passed the cattle and reached the horses, they slowed down.

"All the cows and oxen are lying down, and the horses and mules are standing up," she murmured.

"Our horses haven't lain down since Ohio," William said.

"When I get my horse, I'll teach him to lie down at night."

"Why? They stand because they can run away quicker. That's a horse's best defense."

"But what if they are against a canyon wall and can't run?"

"Then they turn their kickin' end to the enemy and fight."

When they reached the first wagon, William opened the flap of the white canvas tent for her but remained outside. The colonel's bright lantern caused Retta to squint.

The first voice she heard was soft and familiar. "Darlin', come over here for a minute."

She scooted in next to her father. His arm draped around her shoulder, and she reached up and held his fingers.

Colonel Graves paced the dirt floor of the tent. "We can't take that risk," he insisted.

"We can't refuse to help," her father replied.

"They haven't asked for help," the colonel reminded him.

"Landers and the others are too stubborn," Mr. Barre declared. "But they are our friends nonetheless."

Bobcat Bouchet shrugged. "It's their trouble, not ours."

"They wallowed in the mud and got stuck to the axles. But they wanted to be on their own. It will dry sooner or later," Colonel Graves insisted.

"But we'll be two days past them by then. Ten wagons and a few men on horseback on the prairie will be a tempting target for the Cheyenne and Sioux."

She tugged on her father's sleeve. "What happened, Papa?"

"The California-bound need us to help them pull out of the mud. It will cost us another day."

"But then we'll be back together," she said.

Bobcat fingered his scraggly gray beard. "Only until they want to split off again. We have to know who we can count on."

Retta stepped in front of her father. "I can count on Joslyn. She stayed right by me when Tall Owl came at us."

The colonel stopped his pacing. "Young lady, that's what we need to talk to you about."

Bouchet stepped over by her side. "Missy, how many horses did your friends, the Shoshone, have, and what did they look like?"

"Two Bears said he had twelve horses, but I only saw eleven. There were four stallions—two grays, one buckskin, and a black. There were five mares—a sorrel who looked like she was heavy with foal, two duns, and two blue-gray smoky-looking ones. The sorrel had a bad knee, but she had a kind face. There was a one-year-old pinto colt. He was sort of palomino on white and had a very arrogant manner. And there was an old horse that had eyes like a gelding. He was sort of dun-colored with tiger stripes on the back of his front legs and a dark line down his back; so I reckon he had some wild Spanish pony in him."

All three men gaped at her.

She glanced up at her father. "Did I say something wrong?"

Bouchet burst out laughing. "Missy, that's the best description of a remuda I ever heard."

Her father slipped his arm around her. "When did you get to look at all the horses?"

"When I was in the cave, staying out of the rain. I was trying to decide which horse I would want to have as my own . . . you know, if I was to get a horse."

"And which did you pick?" the colonel asked.

Retta held her breath and puffed out her cheeks.

"Well, darlin'?" Her father nudged her.

She bit her lip. "None of them. I'm going to get a chestnut and white pinto gelding as soon as I have enough money." She rocked back on her heels. "Is that all you needed to know?"

"Yep. Missy, you're a jewel!" Bobcat blurted out. "Why, if you were forty years older, I'd marry you on the spot."

"If this young lady were forty years older, she'd have been married for thirty-five years," the colonel pointed out.

"That's true," Bobcat said.

"What's all this about, Papa?"

"Mr. Bouchet found tracks of two dozen or so Indian ponies between here and the California-bound."

"But it wasn't your friends, because all of these ponies had big prints like northern horses."

"The Arapaho?" she asked.

"More than likely." Bouchet nodded. "Course, up in this land it could be Cheyenne or even Sioux."

"It wasn't Two Bears," she maintained. "He wanted to hide from the Arapaho. He wouldn't leave his tracks uncovered."

"You're right there, darlin'," her father replied. "I reckon it was the Arapaho."

"But Tall Owl didn't have a horse," she said.

"He does now. He probably hid it back in the brush, and you didn't see it," Colonel Graves declared.

"Then why was he on foot?" Bobcat mused.

"Without a weapon," Mr. Barre added.

"He did have a big knife," Retta said. She leaned her head back on her father's chest. "Is two dozen a lot of Indians?"

"It's a lot of horses but not necessarily a lot of Indians." Colonel Graves paced again, his right hand resting on the grip of his revolver. "It depends on whether they are an advance party or just travelin' with family or stole some horses from another wagon train."

"If any of the Arapaho are on foot, and they can't find Missy's Indians, they will come here to steal a pony or two," Bobcat warned.

"Or attack the California-bound," Mr. Barre added. "We've got to catch up with them."

"I know you're right, Eugene. But it's the last time we hold up this train," Colonel Graves said. "They have to know that if they pull out again, we won't bail them out."

"Sounds reasonable," Mr. Barre replied. "But when it comes to women and children, I'm not very reasonable."

"You stop and help ever'body, Barre, and you'll never make Oregon before the snow," Bouchet asserted.

Eugene Barre hugged his daughter. "A man's got to live with his conscience, so I reckon we'll stop and help any that are in danger."

When the meeting broke up, Retta clutched her father's arm as they hiked back down the line to their own wagon.

"Aren't the stars beautiful tonight, Papa?"

"I reckon they are, darlin'. I've been too distracted to notice."

"Do you think the stars will look as pretty in Oregon as they do out here on the plains?"

"I reckon Oregon might have the best view of stars in the world. That is, when it isn't raining."

"You really think it rains a lot there?"

"Just enough to keep the crops growing all summer."

"I look forward to getting to Oregon, Papa."

"And I look forward to the sun comin' up in the mornin'."

"Oh, Papa, the sun will come up. It always does."

"And I'm grateful to the Lord ever' mornin'." He paused by the wagon tongue that stretched out empty, like a spacer between wagons. "Did Mama go to bed early?"

"I think so," Retta replied.

"How was she feelin'?"

"She said she was tired, Papa. But she did seem more chipper tonight."

"I figured the talk of more Indians might touch her off again."

"Not nearly as much as it did Mrs. Wilson," Retta said. "She started sucking in her breath and fanning her face, and she got the hiccups and couldn't stop for a long time."

Mr. Barre pulled off his flat-brimmed felt hat and rubbed his chin. "That does sound serious. Is Lerryn up in the wagon with Mama?"

"I think so."

"Take a peek for me."

Retta climbed up in the wagon. The lamp had burned down to such a dim glow that it made the wagon interior look like a distant dream. Mrs. Barre slept fully clothed under the heavy quilt, sweat rolling down her face.

"Is Lerryn with Mama?" Mr. Barre whispered.

Retta stuck her head out. "Papa, she may have gone to Mrs. Ferdinand's wagon."

"My, how that girl likes to sew, just like her mama. They are two peas in a pod, aren't they?" Even in the dim light outside the covered wagon, she could see him smile. "How is everything in there?"

"Mama's sleeping. I'll be here if she needs anything."

"Thanks, darlin'. And tell big sis to relax a little. She doesn't have to sew day and night."

Retta brushed her thick hair back over her ears and watched her father disappear into the darkness. *Papa, I'm not sure what my sister's doing right now, but I don't reckon she's sewing.*

Three

The air inside the covered wagon was slightly cool and stale. Retta could smell Lerryn's perfume, axle grease, and wet earth.

Mainly wet earth.

She climbed over two pine crates and Great-grandma Cutler's old trunk to her mother's side. She tugged down the quilt to where her mother's dress tightened around her stomach and studied the sleeping face. *Lord, Mama's been worried sick ever since Papa told us we were going to Oregon last Christmas. I don't think her heart has ever really been in it. She worries so. And lately she can hardly pull herself around. She sleeps so much. Her face is puffy. She cries at night. I hear her, Lord, but there's nothing I can do for her. Papa said Oregon would be a whole new life. Still, I liked our old life.*

Retta hunted for a linen towel and climbed out of the wagon. Propping up the wooden lid on the water keg that hung on the side of the wagon, she dipped the end of the towel into the water and wrung it out.

"Hi, Retta!"

She spun around to see a boy approach in the darkness. "Oh . . . Ben, hi!"

"What're you doin'?" he asked.

"Getting a wet rag for my mama's face. What're you doing?"

"I'm goin' back to our wagon. I was visitin'."

"How is Ansley tonight?" Retta questioned.

He scratched his head. "To tell you the truth, she's kind of pickled."

"Who is she pickled at?"

"You, of course."

"Me? I always try to avoid Ansley. What did I do?"

"It's 'cause you're the talk of the camp."

"I thought the camp was talking about the Indians and those California-bound wagons."

"They are, but if they talk about anyone our age, they talk about that Barre girl who traded with the Indians," Ben reported.

"And Ansley doesn't like that?"

"No, especially since you took us with you and didn't include her. She's about as happy as a butterfly in brine."

"Ha! Ansley has never wanted to do anything with me in her life," Retta replied.

Ben leaned his right arm against the wagon box. "She does now. Maybe we could take her to see your Indian sometime."

Retta scooted back a little. *We? My Indian? Yeah, if I work real hard, I can make sure she likes you, Ben Weaver. Is that it?*

"What do you say, Retta? Can Ansley come with us next time?"

"Eh, sure," she mumbled.

"Oh, boy!" He patted her shoulder. "You're a real pal. I'm goin' to go tell Ansley right now."

Retta leaned her head back against the wooden box of the big wagon. *I don't know what to do, Lord, but that wasn't it. I don't even know why it matters so much to me anyway. Some days I almost hate Ansley, and some days I think the two of us are an awful lot alike, except that she's cute, and I'm pumpkin-seed plain. If I were fancy like Ansley, I probably would be just as mean as she is.*

The wet rag dribbled between her fingers as she climbed back up into the wagon. Her hands brushed along the rough wooden seat. When she climbed inside, the air still hung heavy. A fly buzzed above her.

She crawled over the crates to her mother's side. "Mama?" she whispered. "Do you want me to wipe your face?"

Mrs. Barre continued to sleep with labored breathing.

Retta gently began to wipe her mother's face. She studied the older woman's light brown hair.

Mama, you have more gray hair than when we left home. Papa says I give you gray hair sometimes. I don't do it on purpose. Your eyes look so tired all the time. I'm glad you're sleeping. The wrinkles are so deep at your eyes.

She dabbed at her mother's neck. The top two buttons of Mrs. Barre's dark green dress were unfastened, exposing a gold locket. Retta fingered the small oval locket. *Inside are those funny little wedding portraits—Mama in one and Papa in the other. Neither of them smiled. Mama said she was too nervous to smile. Papa said he was told it was frivolous to smile in a portrait. Mama says she wouldn't trade that little locket for all the gold in California. I wonder, Lord, if I will ever wear a little locket like that? And whose picture will be in there with mine? Maybe Papa will let me carry his picture.*

She heard the big fly buzz at the top of the wagon, and she tried to spy it in the flickering light. She had just caught sight of it when the fly swooped down and landed on her mother's sweaty forehead.

She brushed it off. "Go on," she whispered. "Go on. You have a whole empty prairie out there to bother. Shoo!"

Retta washed her mother's face again and twice more swatted at the fly. The next time it landed, she tried grabbing it in her hand.

Papa can catch them . . . and so can William. Andrew claps right above them and gets them to fly right into his hands every time. Lerryn won't touch them. Neither will Mama.

I can touch them. I bet I can get this one. Come on, fly. Just light somewhere.

Retta laid the damp rag over her mother's forehead and closed eyes. Then she watched as the big fly lit on her mother's shoulder and crawled toward the locket. Retta held her hands about six inches apart above the locket, as if to clap.

Come on, fly . . . come on . . . just a few more steps.

The fly crawled up on the gold locket just as Mrs. Barre's head rolled to the side, her mouth open.

The fly bolted.

Retta clapped hard.

Mrs. Barre reached up for the rag on her face, and the fly fell from the air.

Oh! I . . . I got it!

"Eugene, I think we need to tell . . ." Mrs. Barre reached her hand to her mouth and coughed.

"It's me, Mama."

"Darlin', thanks for washing my face and . . . Coretta Emily?"

"Did you think it was Lerryn?"

"Yes, I did. But both of my girls are very sweet and thoughtful."

She watched as her mother propped herself up on one elbow and then swallowed hard.

"It's kind of stuffy in here tonight," Mrs. Barre declared.

"Do you want me to open the flap?" Retta offered.

"No, baby. Some of those nasty bugs might come in. You know how I hate bugs. Thank you for taking care of me. I should be awake and taking care of you. It's time for bed. Where's your sis?"

"I don't know."

"I don't like her going off at night with Indians close by. You know what happened to those Oatman girls."

"Do you want me to go hunt for her?"

"No, baby. Your sister is very cautious. She isn't adventuresome like you."

"I imagine she's having an adventure right now," Retta mumbled.

"Is it cloudy outside?" Mrs. Barre asked.

"No, Mama, the stars are very, very pretty."

"That's funny. I can almost taste the sulfur in the air before a lightning strike."

I don't think that's sulfur you're tasting, Mama.

"What were you clapping about when I woke up?"

"I was, eh, chasing a fly off your locket."

"Good. You need to finish the job. There's a huge dead fly on this side of the quilt."

"There is?" Retta shouted and peeked over her mother's rounded stomach to see a huge horsefly lying motionless on the quilt. "Oh, yes! There it is. I'll get it, Mama." She scooped up the horsefly in her hand, crawled over the crates to the front of the wagon, and tossed the dead insect out into the night. *Fly, you had me really, really worried! I thought you went into Mama's mouth.*

Retta felt a hand on her shoulder. She reached up and clutched it. Even in the predawn darkness, she knew the strong, gentle touch.

"Mornin', Papa," she whispered.

In the distance, a gunshot signaled 4:00 A.M. Retta sat up.

"Get us a fire goin', darlin'. William's goin' to yoke the oxen. Andrew will drive the cows and horses to the river for one last drink."

Retta could hear her mother's labored breathing. "Do you want me to wake Mama and Lerryn?"

"Let them sleep until you can see from one end of the wagon to the other. Neither of them can get up without studyin' a mirror for a while."

"Do I need a mirror, Papa?" Retta asked.

"Darlin', you're just as cute as you can be."

Retta giggled. "It's root-cellar-black in here, Papa. You can't even see me."

"You sound cute. I'll be back. Take care of things here."

"You can count on me, Papa."

"I know I can, darlin'. That's why I woke you up."

Retta's brown dress felt stiff and dusty as she pulled it over her head. *Mama's right. When we get to Oregon, we will have to burn all our clothes and make new ones. Except for my buckskin dress. I know I should have her wash this one, but she's not feeling up to it.*

The west wind rolled into camp. Retta tugged her father's old flannel shirt from under the front seat of the wagon and pulled it on over her dress. A lamp was setting on the bucket near the wagon wheel.

She spied shadows in front of the wagon. "Good morning, William," she called out softly as he approached.

"Hi, Retta. How's Mama?"

"Still sleeping. Was there any sign of Indians last night?"

"Lots of wolves howling," Andrew reported.

"Are there wolves around here?"

"I don't think so. That's the point."

"I'll be glad to get back on the trail. Do you reckon the Arapaho will follow us?"

He raised his arm and rubbed his shoulder. "Yep. Why not?"

"I wonder if we'll be allowed to go out and pick up chips," she pondered.

"I reckon they're still too wet."

"Can I borrow the lamp to get the fire started?"

"Sure. I can do this in the dark."

Retta set the lamp on the dirt next to the wagon. The canvas awning was rolled up and stored. The only things left out were the pot hooks, a coffeepot, and a cast-iron skillet with three short legs. She rubbed her eyes and brushed back her bangs and then sorted through the chip sling for the driest ones.

Fire glowed hot under the coffeepot by the time daylight rolled across the prairie. Lerryn mumbled something when she crawled out and plodded off to milk the cows. Retta climbed back up into the wagon.

She put her hand on her mother's cheek. "Mama, it's time to get up," she whispered.

Mrs. Barre opened her eyes. "Morning, Coretta Emily." She sat up and let the quilt drop to her lap. "Whew . . . I do feel better than last night. Hand me my brush and hand mirror, would you, baby?"

Retta crawled over a crate of linens and grabbed the mirror. "Here, Mama. Do you think I need to brush my hair?"

Mrs. Barre began to brush Retta's hair. "Lerryn got back late, didn't she?"

"I think so. I was asleep."

"Did you have to wake her up?"

"I just kind of banged on the coffeepot until she stirred."

"And I didn't hear you?"

"You must have been very, very tired, Mama. I have the fire going and the coffee started."

Mrs. Barre patted her daughter's shoulder. "You're a jewel, Coretta Emily. Ever since we left Ohio, you've made my life easier, and I will always be grateful to the Lord for sending you to me."

"Mama, that's the nicest thing anybody ever said to me."

Mrs. Barre hugged Retta and then shooed her out of the wagon. "Now go on, darlin', before I start to blubber. You know how emotional I've been lately."

Retta scampered to the front of the wagon. "I love you, Mama."

"That did it, young lady. Now I have to find my handkerchief."

Retta climbed out of the wagon in time to greet Ben Weaver and Travis Lott.

Travis tipped his hat. "Good mornin', Miss Barre!"

Retta held the skirt of her worn brown dress and curtsied. "Mornin', Master Lott."

"Well, aren't you two bein' formal!" Ben hooted.

"Travis always treats me like a lady."

"A lady?" Ben laughed.

Retta raised her chin. "Yes."

"Speaking of ladies, have you seen Ansley?" Ben asked.

"She's only a few months older than me."

"Yeah, but she looks . . ." Ben cleared his throat. "Mr. MacGregor said you and Ansley headed out at daybreak."

"I haven't seen Ansley since yesterday. What do you mean, headed out?"

"He said you promised to take her to see your Indian before we pulled out this morning," Travis reported.

"I didn't promise any such thing. Ansley hasn't said anything to me in a couple of days. Nothing nice anyway."

"I wonder why Mr. MacGregor thought that?" Ben puzzled.

"Maybe it was just Ansley's wishful thinkin'," Travis mumbled. "Anyway, if you see her, tell her we're lookin' for her."

The two boys strolled to the next wagon.

Lord, why do I have to tell Ansley that Ben is looking for her? And I don't know why I have such a tough time liking her. I wish You would help me change my feelings about her. But I really wish You would change Ansley.

Retta was helping her mother cook potato cakes when Mr. MacGregor blustered into their camp. "My daughter's gone. Her horse is gone. You're the only one who knows where she is," he roared.

"What?" Mrs. Barre gasped.

"I'm talkin' to your daughter, woman."

Julia Barre waved a long-handled wooden spoon at the man. "You will not talk to me or my daughter in such a voice."

MacGregor rubbed his thick red beard. "You're right, Mrs. Barre, and my apologies. I'm just a worried daddy. Ansley took off and left word she was goin' with your daughter . . . eh . . . eh . . ."

"Her name is Coretta."

"Yeah. Coretta was takin' her to meet that Indian."

"I haven't seen Ansley, Mr. MacGregor. And I never said I'd take her to see Two Bears. He moved camp. I don't even know where he is," Retta explained.

"Retta, come up here!" The shout silenced the camp.

"Your papa wants you," Mrs. Barre said. "Go on." She turned to Mr. MacGregor. "Andrew drove the cattle to the river this morning at daybreak. Perhaps Ansley went to the river."

"Not without my permission," he puffed.

"Wherever she is, it seems she's there without your permission," Mrs. Barre replied.

Retta trotted up the row of wagons to where Bobcat Bouchet stood next to her father. Both men cradled rifles.

"Is that your pal?" Bobcat pointed across the prairie to a brown-skinned man squatted down next to a yucca plant on the rise of a hill.

"That's Two Bears! What's he doing out there?"

"That's exactly what we need you to find out," her father explained.

"Me?"

"He trusts you."

"I'll come with you," Bobcat stated.

Retta waved at the man out on the prairie. "Not with a gun in your hand. He doesn't trust men with guns."

Four

Two Bears was hunched down on the prairie near a lone yucca that had tall grass growing up through it, his red bandanna tied around his forehead. He held an arrow in one hand and scratched in the dirt with it, but Retta couldn't see a bow. He pointed the arrow at them but remained hunkered down.

"Who is with you, Red Bear?"

Retta stopped, laced her fingers, and rested them on top of her head. "He's our scout, Mr. Bobcat Bouchet."

Two Bears showed no emotion. "Does he have a gun?"

Retta glanced over at Bouchet. He held out his arms and hands.

"No," she reported.

She thought Two Bears's eyes looked sad. "I want to speak to you alone," he mumbled.

Retta curled her lip and rubbed her round nose but didn't walk any closer. "He wanted to meet you."

Bouchet stroked his tobacco-stained beard. "I'm a friend of Jim Bridger's."

Two Bears began to draw in the dirt with the arrow again. "I never heard of you."

Bobcat Bouchet shoved his hat back. "Two Bears, I was with ol' Gabe when the Blackfeet hit us up on Prickly Pear Creek near the divide."

The Indian looked up. "Who died that day?"

"Seven Blackfeet, Big Tom Smith, and a stout Shoshone we called Leonard," Bouchet reported.

Two Bears scratched behind his ear with the tip of the arrow. "He was my cousin."

Bouchet took a couple of steps forward. "He was a brave man. He had an ugly-lookin' scar over his right eye."

Two Bears's leather-tough face relaxed a bit. "I was with him the day he got that scar." He glanced at Retta. "Your friend is okay, Red Bear. He can come with you."

When they reached Two Bears, both Retta and Bouchet squatted down in front of him. She glanced at the ground and saw the image of a hawk with a mouse in its talons scratched in the dirt.

The smile dropped off Two Bears's face. He ignored Bouchet and spoke to Retta. "Have you seen my Shy Bear?"

"No, I haven't." Retta drew in the dirt with her finger. "Is she lost?"

Two Bears jabbed the arrow into the chest of the hawk in the dirt. "She is not lost. Shy Bear knows her way. She might be where she does not want to be, but that does not make her lost. She wanted to come see you. She slipped out of camp early riding the old gelding."

Retta erased her scribbles in the dirt. "Why did she want to come see me?"

"She felt bad that you had given her the nice hat, but she did not give you anything."

Retta shook her head. "But—but I have her beautiful dress. It's more than enough."

"She wanted to give you an eagle feather and a beaded headband she made." He sketched a feather in the dirt.

"My own eagle feather? Oh, that would be wonderful!" Retta started to draw a feather but ended up drawing a cross.

"I told her I would bring the headband to you when it was safe and the Arapaho had left. But she was afraid you would leave, and she wouldn't get to see you. Her trail led near the river and then was trampled on by the cows. I can't follow it further."

"One of our girls is missing too," Retta informed him.

Bobcat Bouchet rocked back on his heels. "Who? I hadn't heard that."

"Ansley MacGregor, the red-headed girl on the black horse." Retta tried to draw a horse in the firm, wet soil.

Two Bears reached over and erased her drawing with his fingers.

"Where did she go?" Bouchet asked.

"She told her papa that her and me were coming to see Two Bears, but I never saw her this morning. I wasn't going anywhere. I didn't even know where Two Bears was camping."

"Do you think she is where she does not want to be?" Two Bears asked.

"Either that or she's just plain lost." Retta bit her lip and nodded. "She doesn't know her way around very well."

Bobcat pulled out a clay pipe and chewed on the stem. "Sounds like we have two missing girls. I wonder if they could be together."

"Maybe," Retta said. "But Ansley isn't very brave. I think she would be frightened of Shy Bear."

"No one has ever been frightened of Shy Bear. I was very surprised that she left camp on her own," Two Bears said.

"You thinkin' maybe that Arapaho nabbed them?" Bouchet asked.

Two Bears drew a hill under Retta's cross. "I do not want to think about that, but it might be."

"We found tracks of Indian horses between here and the California-bound wagons up there," Bouchet volunteered.

Two Bears rubbed his chin. "Horses? That is strange. Tall Owl did not have a horse. We tracked him into the brush, and there was no horse."

Bouchet stared off into the tall brown grass far to the south of the wagons. "If he joined up with others, he has a horse now."

"But why did he not have a horse when I saw him? A famous Arapaho warrior without a horse is a strange thing," Two Bears puzzled.

"Maybe he rode him down," Retta suggested. "Or the horse lamed up."

"Only if Tall Owl was chased. Who would be chasing him? You see, it is a mystery."

Retta watched as Two Bears drew a small cross to the right of her large one. "What does this have to do with Ansley and Shy Bear?" she asked.

The Indian then drew a third cross to the left of hers. "Maybe that band of Indians is after Tall Owl."

Bobcat rocked back on his heels. "Why? Why would Arapaho be chasin' an Arapaho?"

"Maybe there are other tribes in the area." Two Bears drew a sun in the dirt about the three crosses. "Did they steal any horses last night?"

"No, not a sign of them," Bouchet reported. "But there are some wagons up ahead of us. I haven't gotten a message from them yet."

"They didn't come after me and my family either. It is curious. I am sure they know I am here."

Bobcat spoke. "Looks like we've got two girls to look for. Maybe we should join up."

Two Bears studied Bouchet and then Retta. "Yes, that would be good. We will join with you, provided Red Bear comes. She is part of my family." He reached out for her hand.

Retta immediately took his hand. It was strong and callused, much like her father's.

Two Bears pointed to the three crosses on the hill etched in the wet dirt. "Now Red Bear will pray."

I can't pray out loud. Only with Mama. Lerryn says my prayers are funny. I . . . I . . . Retta cleared her throat. "Lord Jesus, it's me—Retta . . . eh, Coretta Emily Barre. This is my friend Two Bears. I guess You know that already. And this is Bobcat Bouchet. He probably has another name, but I don't know what it is. And, Lord, he doesn't mean any disrespect when he cusses at the oxen. He's really nice on the inside once you get to know him, and don't let the tobacco stains on his beard bother you."

"Hehhhhhum." Bobcat cleared his throat.

"Lord, we have a problem. Ansley and Shy Bear aren't exactly lost, but they are somewhere they don't want to be. And we want them to be here. So if You'd keep them safe until we find them, we'd appreciate it, and if I need to do something to help You, well, I'll do it. Especially for Shy Bear. I mean, I'll do it for Ansley, too, but . . . well, she's the red-headed girl I talked to You about last week. So You can see my dilemma. . . . Anyway, I'll talk to You about that later. Bye, Lord . . . eh, in Jesus' name, amen."

Bobcat jammed his hat back on.

Two Bears trotted toward the tall grass to the south, packing the arrow and grinning.

The oxen were yoked, mules harnessed, horses saddled and standing ready by the time Retta pulled on her buckskin dress and moccasins and rejoined Colonel Graves and her father near the lead wagon. Within a matter of minutes, the bugle sounded, and the wagons were rolling west. As they did, a small band of riders trotted out to the yucca plant on the hill.

To come along with Two Bears and his two sons, Retta chose Bobcat Bouchet, her father, her brother William, Mr. Weaver, and old Sven Neilsen, the best shot in the wagon train. Hugh MacGregor had insisted on coming, too.

MacGregor's thick red beard brushed out from under his hat as he pointed at Two Bears. "How do we know this Indian is not leadin' us into an ambush?"

Retta puffed out her cheeks. "Because his daughter is missing, too!"

"I wasn't talking to you," he growled. "It's your fault my daughter's lost—yours and this fool Indian's. If you had stayed with the wagons where you belong and not gotten that savage's dress, none of this would have happened."

Eugene Barre trotted his buckskin next to MacGregor, grabbed the headstall on his horse, and jerked it around. "Listen to me, MacGregor, and listen carefully. You have a missin' daughter, and me and my boy and my girl are puttin' our lives on the line to help find her. Don't you ever use that tone of voice with my daughter again. I won't tolerate it for a minute."

MacGregor rested his thumb on the big hammer of his rifle. "Are you threatenin' me?"

Mr. Barre shoved the barrel of his gun into MacGregor's midsection. "You better believe I am!"

Retta could feel her heart pound.

"Look!" Two Bears called out. "We have company!"

Retta let her breath out slowly as she studied the northern horizon. Several mounted men rode through the brush near the river. *Lord, I . . . I almost got my papa into a shooting match with Mr. MacGregor. I didn't cause Ansley to ride off and get into trouble . . . did I?*

"I reckon those are the Arapaho," Bobcat declared.

"No," Two Bears replied. "It is the Cheyenne."

"Cheyenne?" Retta gulped.

"Now we have stirred up a hornet's nest," Bouchet mumbled. "If the Cheyenne are in on it, the Sioux can't be far behind."

"It looks like they want to talk," Two Bears observed.

Even though the morning sun was behind her, Retta shaded her eyes and stared at the men on the horses. "How can you tell they want to talk?"

Two Bears dismounted. "Because they are out in the open, and they didn't charge at us or shoot at us."

Hugh MacGregor cocked the massive hammer back on his rifle. "Hidin' in the trees ain't exactly what I'd call bein' out in the open."

Bouchet slid down out of his saddle, rifle in hand. "For the Cheyenne, it is."

"I say we shoot 'em all!" MacGregor growled.

"What will that do for your daughter?" Sven Neilsen challenged.

"Revenge." MacGregor started to raise his rifle to his shoulder.

Mr. Weaver reached over and held the gun down. "Revenge for what, Hugh? We don't know where your daughter is. Or how she is. We don't even know if these Indians have anything to do with her. Besides, Ansley could be back at the wagon train by now. Don't be a fool and jeopardize all our lives."

Two Bears squatted down and stared across at the Cheyenne. "We must go halfway to them. There are three of them. There must be three of us," he explained.

"I reckon I'd better go," Bouchet said, "since I know a little of the language. And Two Bears and one other."

"I'm going," MacGregor snarled.

"Not with a gun," Bouchet objected.

"If they harmed my daughter, I'll kill them with my bare hands."

"No," Two Bears insisted. "Red Bear must be the third."

"Who in blazes is Red Bear?" MacGregor fumed.

"That's me," Retta declared.

"This ain't no matter for a little girl," MacGregor growled.

Retta bit her lip. "I'm almost thirteen."

"Why does my daughter have to go?" Mr. Barre asked.

"If they see Red Bear with us, they will know we aren't looking for a fight. Cheyenne do not trust anyone," Two Bears explained.

William pulled off his wire-framed spectacles and rubbed the bridge of his nose. "But what if the Cheyenne are lookin' for a fight?"

"Then they would be shooting at us now and have no reason to talk. They want something from us," Bobcat said.

"There's only three of them," MacGregor pointed out.

"Only three that can be seen. They are not fools," Two Bears informed him. "They would not reveal their position unless they had the strength to oppose us."

Retta slipped off her horse and brushed down her buckskin skirt.

"Be careful, darlin'," her father cautioned.

"Papa, me, Two Bears, and Mr. Bouchet have already prayed and asked for the Lord's hand to be with us today."

"Bobcat prayed?" Mr. Weaver exclaimed.

"Ever'body prays, Weaver," Bobcat snorted. He spat a wad of tobacco on the dirt by his boots and wiped his beard on the sleeve of his shirt.

The three hiked across the prairie toward the Indians. Retta lagged behind. When they got about halfway, Two

Bears squatted down and drew circles in the damp soil. Bobcat and Retta hunkered down next to him.

The three Indians who came toward them were taller than Two Bears, broad-shouldered, and shirtless. Their straight black hair hung halfway to their waists. One had horrible ragged horizontal scars on his upper chest. All three wore buckskin leggings, loin cloths, moccasins, and beaded headbands with a single eagle feather drooping across their ears. One wore a gold cross on a braided horsehair string.

They squatted down across from Two Bears and spoke so rapidly that Retta could not even tell when one word ended and another began. Two Bears answered them in the same language.

She leaned over to Bobcat and whispered, "What did they say?"

He rubbed his beard so that his hand shielded his mouth. "I think they asked who we are," he whispered back.

"What did Two Bears tell them?"

Bobcat pulled off his hat and held it over his mouth. "He said me and him were scouts for the wagon train. Then he said you were his daughter."

"His daughter?"

"You got dark hair and a dress of buckskin. You don't wear a bonnet like the other girls, and your face is as tanned as a trapper's. Havin' his daughter along shows peaceful intent."

She cupped her hands over her mouth and whispered, "Why did he tell them he was a scout?"

Bouchet's voice dropped even lower. "I reckon he didn't want to tell them he has a family hidin' in the brush."

The Cheyenne with scars on his chest pulled a pansy-plum gingham garment from his belt.

"That's my bonnet!" Retta whispered. "I mean, the one I gave to Shy Bear."

"Don't look surprised," Bouchet warned. "Show no emotions."

"What?"

Bobcat nodded at the Shoshone. "Be like Two Bears."

Retta studied Two Bears's quiet face. He looked as if he were about to fall asleep. "What did they just say?"

"They're looking for Tall Owl, the Arapaho," Bouchet replied.

"Why?" Retta asked.

Bouchet drew an arrow in the dirt with his finger. "He killed someone." He paused to listen to the Arapaho. "My word, Missy, he done killed a Cheyenne medicine man!"

Retta studied the darting brown eyes of the Cheyenne speaker. "You mean, they are after Tall Owl and not the wagon train?"

"I reckon so."

"What about the bonnet? Where did they get it? Do they know where Shy Bear is?"

Bouchet listened for several moments. "They found it near the river this mornin', but our remuda muddied the trail. They had followed Tall Owl here and lost him in the brush. He was on foot at first, but later they found horse tracks. They think Tall Owl now has two horses. They want to know who the bonnet belongs to."

"Two horses? You think he has the ones Ansley and Shy Bear were riding?"

"That's what I surmise," Bobcat muttered. "Two Bears told them there are two girls missing from the wagon train, and we would not stop until we got them back."

"Is the bonnet torn?" Retta asked.

Two Bears continued to talk to the Cheyenne, but he handed the bonnet back to her.

She turned it over in her hand. "It isn't muddy. It looks like it was merely dropped."

"Two Bears said the girl with the bonnet was very smart and probably left it for a trail to follow. He said to look for other signs."

"What kind of signs?"

"He didn't say."

Retta pulled the bonnet over her head.

Bobcat Bouchet rubbed his whiskers. "They said Tall Owl is very mean and, well, I think they said unpredictable. Somethin' about him bein' like an animal that has gone mad."

Retta puffed out her cheeks. "That's horrible. What will happen to Ansley and Shy Bear?"

The three Cheyenne men looked at Retta and laughed.

"Are they laughing at me?"

"Yes. They say a hat like that looks silly on a Shoshone girl like you."

"But it was my bonnet."

"They're convinced you belong to Two Bears."

"Will Tall Owl hurt Ansley and Shy Bear?" she asked.

"The Cheyenne said that out here on his own, Tall Owl will probably use them to barter for supplies."

"What're we going to do?"

Bobcat pulled out his clay pipe and chewed on the stem. "Well, I'll be . . ."

"What is it?"

"Your Indian said we should join forces with the Cheyenne and find the man and the girls together."

"Join forces with the Cheyenne?"

"They'll take one side of the river, and we'll take the other. We'll ride northwest until we flush out Tall Owl."

"What happens when we find him?"

"We get the girls; they get him."

The Cheyenne stood. Two Bears nodded. He, Bouchet, and Retta stood as well.

"How do we know we can trust them?" Retta whispered.

"We don't. Tough to know that. But you saw Tall Owl down by the river. Do you want to side with him?"

Retta shivered.

The Cheyenne crossed the river that was a hundred yards wide and about a foot deep. They fanned out into the overgrowth.

Two Bears and his sons dismounted and scouted the thickest part of the brush. Retta rode behind her father.

"What are we looking for, Papa?"

"Fresh horse prints."

"Won't he ride right in the river?"

"Probably, but sooner or later he'll have to come to shore."

"Why? Can't they go all day in the river?"

"Perhaps, but we should be able to go faster on the shore. We'll catch up."

Retta circled his waist with her hands. "Papa, is this all my fault? I mean, if I hadn't traded for this buckskin dress, neither Ansley nor Shy Bear would be in trouble."

"Nonsense, darlin', you didn't do one thing wrong."

Hugh MacGregor rode up beside them. "I'll shoot that Arapaho on sight if he has my girl."

"Don't shoot until we make sure Ansley and Shy Bear are safe!" Retta urged.

"Don't shoot at all," Bobcat cautioned. "The only way we'll get these Cheyenne to ride off is to give them Tall Owl alive. If we help them, we won't have any future trouble— from this one band, anyway."

Brush moved by the river, but Retta could only see Two Bears and his sons. "At least Tall Owl doesn't have a gun. I didn't see one. So he can't shoot them."

MacGregor pulled off his grimy hat and wiped his forehead. "I'm sure Ansley kept her pistol hidden. She knows how to protect herself."

Retta glanced at Bouchet and back at Mr. MacGregor. "Ansley carries a gun?"

"She's packed a small two-shot pocket pistol for several years."

"I've never seen it," Retta said.

"See? I told you she knows how to keep it concealed."

"That means Tall Owl does have a gun!" Bobcat exclaimed.

"Nonsense. She wouldn't surrender it," MacGregor insisted.

"That's the silliest statement I ever heard. You can bet Tall Owl has it."

"He would search a young girl? That's—that's barbaric."

"A man who's being hunted by the Cheyenne will do whatever it takes to survive." Bobcat spurred his horse toward the brush.

"Where're you going?" Retta called out.

"To warn the others that Tall Owl may be carryin' a gun."

"It's merely a two-shot," MacGregor yelled.

"It only takes one well-placed bullet to kill any of us," Bobcat hollered back.

Five

For over an hour Retta strained her eyes to survey the brush, the river, and the empty prairie. Once in a while she could see the Cheyenne and always those on her side of the river, but never Ansley, Shy Bear, the Arapaho, or a scrap of pansy-plum gingham.

Her mind kept drifting to repeated prayer. *Lord, I'm really worried about Ansley. She isn't very wise, and she needs You to protect her. And Shy Bear. . . . They must be scared to death, and I'm wondering what's going to happen to them. Please protect them, Lord. Protect us all. Oh, Jesus, I wish I knew what to do.*

A lone coyote yelp brought the search to a stop. Two Bears stared across the river at the Cheyenne. Several hand signals later, he hurried back to Retta and the others.

"They saw horses ahead in the brush on our side."

"Then what're we waiting for?" MacGregor demanded.

"We gotta find out the condition of the girls first," Bobcat cautioned. "If he's holdin' a knife to their throats, we surely don't want to set him off. We know he has a knife."

"So what do we do?" MacGregor asked. "Ride straight up and ask him?"

"I reckon so," Bobcat replied.

"What do you mean?" Retta's father asked.

"Neilsen and Weaver, go around to the north," Bouchet ordered. "Eugene and his boy should stay to guard the south. Me, Two Bears, MacGregor, and Missy will ride right up to them."

"Why does Retta need to go with you this time?" Mr. Barre demanded.

"Same reason. Because she's merely out looking for her friends. We don't want to look like we're expecting trouble. We're just searchin' for two lost girls. We'll offer to make a trade."

"I won't trade with the savage," MacGregor snarled.

"I will," Two Bears stated as he remounted his horse. "I love my daughter."

MacGregor's wild eyes darted from man to man. "I love my daughter, too. It's just . . ."

"You love your things more?" Two Bears challenged.

"Of course not! But it's not right to let that savage charge us for our own girls."

"Even if we trade, he won't get far, will he?" Mr. Barre put in.

MacGregor rubbed his chin. "You mean, the Cheyenne will nab him?"

"Exactly."

"Well, this is crazy," MacGregor said. "I'm goin' to go get my Ansley!"

Bobcat's face flushed. He waved his hands as he spoke. "We'll take your gun, coldcock you, and tie you to your saddle."

"What?" the big man gulped.

Bouchet rode straight up to him. "MacGregor, we're committed to bringing your daughter out of here alive, a fact that doesn't seem to be in your mind."

MacGregor closed his eyes. "Okay, I'll come along peaceful."

"Good. Now dismount. We're hiking in," Bouchet instructed.

"I'm leading the way," MacGregor insisted.

Bouchet pulled off his hat and resat it on his head. "No, you're the last in line, or you don't go with us at all. Is that understood?"

MacGregor's neck reddened. "If my daughter is harmed, I'll kill him."

"Not with that gun. Give it to me," Bouchet demanded. "You're going to get us all killed."

"I don't surrender my gun to any man."

"Then give it to Missy or stay back here with the others. You're not goin' to carry a gun."

"You're all insane!" MacGregor huffed.

"If your daughter has been harmed, we'll never find the Arapaho. If he wants to negotiate, that means the girls are safe, for now. Well, MacGregor? Are you goin' to give Missy the gun?"

"Of all the wagon trains, I get the only one with a lunatic for a scout." He shoved the gun at Retta.

"Two scouts." Bobcat yanked off his dirty felt hat, folded the brim up in the front, and shoved it onto Two Bears's head. "Now you look like a scout."

Retta walked along with the long muzzle-loading rifle propped over her shoulder. *Lord, this is like a dream—a nightmare. I don't know what I'm doing here. Help me not to do something dumb and get someone hurt. I didn't know this dress would get me into so much trouble. If I hadn't gotten the dress, I'd be sitting back at the wagon with Lerryn, taking care of a sickly mama. And Ansley wouldn't have wandered off seeking Two Bears. Of course, Shy Bear*

*would be safe with her papa, too. Oh, Lord, maybe it is all
my fault.*

Two Bears crept forward into the brush along the river,
followed by Bobcat Bouchet, then Retta, and finally a sulk-
ing Hugh MacGregor. The sun pierced the pale blue sky
above them. Retta heard a hawk screech but couldn't see any
bird. The brush along the river had thickened, and the grass
under her feet still held the morning dew. She could see her
moccasins darken from the moisture, but she didn't feel the
dampness.

When they reached the river, Two Bears motioned them
to squat down. Retta hid behind a bush, leaning on the rifle.
She inched toward Bouchet. "Why did we stop?" she whispered.

"The horses are right up there." He pointed upriver.

She peered over the brush. "I can't see them."

"Nope, but Two Bears can smell them."

"What're we waiting for?" MacGregor grumbled.

Bobcat picked his teeth with his grimy fingernail. "A
sign that Tall Owl wants to negotiate."

"You think he knows we're here?"

"Yep, but if we're lucky, he doesn't know the Cheyenne
are across the river."

"I don't think he knows we're—" MacGregor's mumbling was cut off by a gunshot that sprayed shallow water
next to them. MacGregor lunged for the gun in Retta's hand.

Bouchet's rifle kept the big man at bay. "That was the
signal to palaver."

MacGregor glared at the others. "He tried to kill us."

"No man alive on the prairie is that bad a shot,"
Bouchet insisted. "He missed us on purpose."

Two Bears spun around with a grin. "This is good."

"Good?" MacGregor growled. "A savage killer has my
daughter."

"MacGregor, the point is," Bouchet explained, "that he just wasted one of two shots from your daughter's gun. That means he doesn't know the Cheyenne are on the other side of the river."

"But they know where he is," Retta said.

"And they know he has a gun," Bobcat added.

Retta bit on her lip. "Who goes to negotiate?"

"There is one of him, and so only one can go," Two Bears said.

"I reckon I should go," Bobcat offered, "and leave you two fathers back here. MacGregor is too volatile, and Two Bears faced him down once before. He might not want to see you again."

"I'm goin' after my own daughter," MacGregor insisted.

"Not until we find out her situation," Bobcat warned.

"I will stay here only if Red Bear goes with you," Two Bears said. "She will not be a threat to Tall Owl."

"I slugged him once, remember?" Retta reminded him.

"Yes, and he respects you for that. I believe he will listen to you," Two Bears said.

"Leave the guns here," Bouchet instructed. "With the Cheyenne on one side of the river and Barre, Weaver, and the others here, we have him pinned in. He can't go anywhere." He turned to Retta. "Are you ready?"

"Yes. What am I supposed to do?"

"Look like you're scoutin' for tracks ahead of me," he told her.

"What?"

"You're the Indian, remember? You're supposed to know how to read tracks."

Retta sauntered toward a clearing, her head down, staring at the dirt.

"Squat down and examine the mud," Bobcat whispered.

She squatted as Bouchet hovered over her shoulder.

The brush stirred, and Shy Bear, wearing the pansy-plum dress, emerged with her hands tied behind her. She stared down at the ground and didn't look up.

"Don't say a word," Bobcat ordered.

Ansley was tethered behind Shy Bear, her hands tied behind her back also. "Retta," she said, "tell him to cut me loose right now!"

"Tell her to put her head down and be quiet," Bouchet instructed.

"Get me loose," Ansley pleaded.

"Ansley, please be like Shy Bear," Retta requested. "We have to talk to him first."

She caught a glimpse of Ansley's frightened green eyes before the girl's head dropped.

Tall Owl strutted out behind the bound girls. He mumbled several words and pointed at Retta.

She shielded her mouth with her hand. "What did he say?"

"He said there are too many girls and not enough men."

Bouchet spoke several words to the Indian.

"What did you tell him?"

"That we want the girls back and are willing to trade."

Retta waited for them to finish another round of discussion. She couldn't read anything in Tall Owl's face. "What does he want?" she finally asked.

Bouchet scratched the back of his head. "Bullets, food, and you."

"Me?"

"He said he would trade the two girls for black powder, lead balls, a sack of food, and the Indian girl with the strong fist."

"He thinks I'm an Indian girl?"

"I reckon."

"Why does he want me?"

"He says he has two horses. If you rode ahead of him, he could pass through the land more safely. You have strong arms and could put up his tent for him. Put your head back down and don't show emotion."

"What? I'm being bartered like a slave in Charleston, and I'm not supposed to show emotion? What did you tell him?"

"I told him we would have to go to the wagons for the food and bullets, but that was all he gets. You are a free person and cannot be traded."

"What did he say?"

"He said to ask the free person if she wanted to come because he needs an Indian girl, or he will just keep the two girls he has. He said that if we will not trade, he will look for someone who will."

Ansley MacGregor sobbed.

Retta glanced over at her.

Between gasps Ansley mouthed the words, "Help me! Please, Retta, help me."

Lord, she's terrified. I've never seen Ansley look so scared and pitiful.

Retta puffed out her cheeks for a long moment. Finally she whispered, "Tell him you'll make the trade. I've decided to go with him."

"Missy, this ain't a game. I'm not about to trade you away," Bouchet protested.

"You said we have him surrounded. So he can't go anywhere. The girls will be free. Then in a few minutes so will I. Besides, he won't finish the trade until someone comes back with food."

Bouchet pulled off his hat to shield his face. "You mean, this will be just to stall him?"

"Yes," she whispered.

Bouchet spoke to Tall Owl.

Retta kept her face down and listened to the tone of the Arapaho's voice. She thought she heard it soften.

"What did he say?" she whispered.

Bouchet interpreted for her. "He says to go get the food. He wanted you to stay, but I told him no."

Retta clasped her hands and held them under her chin. Sharp pains throbbed at her temples. *Lord Jesus . . . this is not . . . I don't . . .* "Ask him if I stay, will he let the girls go to their mamas now?" she blurted out.

"I won't let you stay," Bouchet insisted.

She looked over to see Ansley lean her head on Shy Bear's shoulder. Both girls were crying.

"Ask him," Retta demanded.

Bobcat's words were halting. Tall Owl became excited.

"He said he would let one girl go if you stay."

Retta never lifted her head. "No. Both girls must go. What if we give him some black powder and lead balls. Will he let them loose then?"

Bobcat pressed his callused hand on her arm. "Missy, you don't know what you're sayin'."

Retta watched Ansley as her body shook. She squeezed the scout's fingers. "Please ask him!"

There were several more moments of conversation.

"He says he will trade. He's tired of listening to the red-haired one cry. But I'm not goin' to let you do that. That's not why we came in here."

"But we have him surrounded, and the lead balls you carry are for a .45 caliber, not a small caliber. He can't use them in Ansley's gun until he melts them down. Besides, it's sort of my fault they were captured."

"Missy, I couldn't look your papa in the eyes if I let you go with the Arapaho," Bouchet insisted.

"Give me your powder horn and your bullet bag. He only has one bullet that will work in Ansley's gun. Isn't that right?"

"That might be. I don't see the gun," Bouchet replied. "But it only takes one bullet to kill someone."

"I won't try running away. Why would he shoot me? Then he wouldn't have an alibi or someone to set up his tepee. The Lord will protect me," she assured him.

"No, I won't do that—"

Bouchet was interrupted by a shout from the Arapaho.

"What did he say?" Retta asked.

"He said to hurry! He wants to be far from here by sundown."

Retta could hear dry heaves coming from Ansley.

"Give me your powder horn." Retta thrust her arm toward Bobcat.

Bouchet handed her the powder horn and pulled the bullet pouch off his belt. "You're as brave as ol' Jim Bridger himself."

"Mr. Bouchet, that's a very nice compliment. I'm not brave, but I don't think I could live with myself if either of these girls got hurt."

"What will I tell your daddy?"

"Who knows whether I have not come to the kingdom for such a time as this?" she replied.

The scout rubbed his beard. "What?"

"Just say that. Papa will understand. Tell him I'm not afraid."

Retta walked with her head down, carrying the powder and lead balls in front of her. As she approached the bound girls, Ansley wiped her eyes on her sleeve and whispered, "What's going on?"

"Ansley and Shy Bear, walk straight over to Mr. Bouchet."

"But what about my horse?" Ansley whimpered.

"Ansley MacGregor, get out of here before I get too scared to go through with this." Retta glanced at Tall Owl's big gun. "Where did he get that revolver? I thought he had your two-shot .32."

"I took Daddy's spare .45," Ansley replied as she and Shy Bear scurried past Retta.

Tall Owl yanked the powder horn and bullet pouch from Retta's hands and growled something at her.

Retta stood still and stared down at her feet.

Lord, I don't know what I'm doing here. A minute ago this seemed like a reasonable action. Now it seems like a nightmare. I would like to just go back to the wagon and crawl under the quilt and stay there until we get to Oregon.

Tall Owl grunted at her and pointed to the ground. She sat down cross-legged on the dirt.

We would get along much better if you tried to be pleasant. But I can't tell you that because I don't speak Arapaho, and you don't speak English. Why does he want food from the wagon train? He's an Indian. He's used to finding his own food. And why does he think they will come back? They have the girls. Why should they come back if they are trading me anyway? I mean, they will come back. And Papa and William are out there in the brush with the others and will come busting through any second now. But why would Tall Owl think they will return? This is the dumbest plan I ever had in my life, except maybe that time I made a cat raft out of balloons.

Retta watched Tall Owl load powder into the revolver and set the lead balls.

Lord, I think I made a big mistake. I was pretending to be something I'm not. I want to go home now. I'm not brave. I'm not strong. I'm just as scared as Ansley was. He's not going to wait. He's going to take me with him.

When Tall Owl finished loading his gun, he motioned to the bushes behind them and barked a command.

"I really have no idea what you just said. If you would slow down when you talk and try to smile more, perhaps I could find out what you want." *Am I supposed to go into those bushes? Is he going to shoot me now? But why would he shoot me?*

Retta held her breath and puffed out her cheeks.

Tall Owl leaned over her, took his two thumbs, and poked them sharply into her cheeks.

Retta's mouth deflated.

He shouted at her again and pointed to the bushes. She marched to the brush, head down, hands hanging against the buckskin dress.

Why did I want this old dress? It was just a game. I wanted to have something that no one else on the wagon train had. I was very, very foolish. Lord, I really think this would be a good time for Papa and William to come rescue me. I've learned my lesson. I'll stay next to the wagon at all times. I'll help Mama through her sickness. I'll never get mad at Lerryn again. Okay, well, maybe just a few times, but not nearly as often.

She plodded through the brush and glanced over her shoulder. *I wonder why he's not following me? Maybe I can run away. But he knows that. Maybe he wants me to run away so he can shoot me. But why would he trade two girls for one and then shoot her?*

She looked up. Four big brown eyes stared back at her. *The horses. That's it. He wants me to bring the horses! We're leaving. But we're surrounded, aren't we? And Papa and Mr. Bouchet and Two Bears will be here soon and the others and then . . . then . . .*

Retta untied both horses. Ansley's long-legged black horse pranced at the reins. Shy Bear's horse nuzzled against Retta's arm.

"How are you, boy?" she whispered. "Don't worry, we are completely surrounded, and I'll have you back to Shy Bear soon."

When she returned to the clearing, Retta kept her head down. On his knees in the dirt, Tall Owl rolled his powder horn and bullets in a scrap of deer hide painted with a crude crescent moon and some stars.

"Here are the horses. I don't know which one you want to ride, but I suppose Ansley's."

He snatched the reins of the black horse from her hands.

Do I walk behind his horse? Do I ride? Is this my horse? Lord, I don't know the rules. This would be a very good time for Papa to show up.

Retta stood and watched as Tall Owl tied his belongings on the back of Ansley's tooled-leather saddle. He retied the cinch and then scooted around to the off-side of the horse. With ease he swung himself up in the saddle.

The moment his buckskin breeches hit the saddle leather, the horse dropped his head, kicked out his hind feet, twisted to the right, crashed to the ground, and bucked back up in the air.

Tall Owl mounted on the wrong side. Ansley's horse doesn't like anyone climbing up the off-side. Ben told me that one time! Tall Owl must have thought that he's an Indian pony like Shy Bear's horse.

The Indian stayed on board as the long-legged horse bucked along the river's edge. He tried to steer the horse out into the river, but the black horse spun back, dropped his head, lost his footing, and then leaped straight up. When the horse came down, his feet slipped on the rocks, and his rider went flying.

Retta stood frozen at the sight. *I should run away. I need to run. He might shoot me.*

Tall Owl landed on his back in six-inch-deep water along the river's edge in a partly submerged rock field. He lay still for a moment.

Retta puffed out her cheeks and held her breath. Her voice was weak. "Are you hurt, Tall Owl?"

Finally the Indian pulled himself to his feet.

She glanced back down at hers.

He seemed more subdued. He motioned to her to mount the other horse.

Retta started for the left side of Shy Bear's horse, then paused, and scooted over to the right side. *An Indian pony. Mount on the off-side. I hope.*

She grabbed the horse's dark mane and leaped toward his back, landing on her stomach. She struggled to get both of her legs on the same side of the horse so she could keep the buckskin skirt pulled down past the top of her moccasins.

When she turned the horse around, Tall Owl led Ansley's horse back to the clearing. He dried his wet hands on his long, thick, shiny black hair and took a deep breath.

He's going to try it from the off-side again! "No!" Retta called out, pointing to the left side of the horse. "He bucks when you try to mount up from over there."

He glared at her and started to mount.

"No!" she warned.

She had no idea what he said back to her, but she knew he was mad.

He shoved his foot into the right side stirrup.

Retta puffed out her cheeks.

As soon as his left leg swung over the saddle, the tall

black horse began to buck. This time he snorted as he dropped his head and whinnied as he tossed it back. After three wild bucks, he reached the water's edge. He yanked his head forward, pulling Tall Owl down over his head. Then he jerked his head straight back, slamming it into Tall Owl's forehead.

The collision exploded like the bursting of a barn board in a tornado. Tall Owl tumbled facedown into the shallow water, hit his head on a rock, and didn't move. The pony scurried back to the little clearing.

Retta dropped straight down off her horse and let the reins fall to the ground. She ran over to the Indian. "Tall Owl? Popa?"

Lord, is he dead? He will be if his head stays underwater. It was an accident. He's a very mean man, but . . .

She waded out and tugged on his arm until she rolled him on his back. Retta took a flat rock and propped it under the back of his head, raising his face above water. Then she yanked the soaking-wet revolver out of his belt and removed the big knife from the sheath at his side.

I wonder if this powder got too wet to fire?

Retta used both thumbs to tug back the hammer of the .45-caliber revolver and pointed it in the air.

There was a loud, disappointing click.

She cocked it again with the same result.

She popped two fingers in her mouth to whistle, then paused, and cocked the gun again. This time when she pulled the trigger, the gun blast exploded above her head. She dropped the gun, stumbled back, and sprawled on her rear in the shallow water. She held the big knife straight out in front of her as she heard someone running toward her out of the brush.

Six

William crashed through the brush and reached her first. "Retta! Are you hurt?"

Mr. Barre raced past him and scooped her out of the water with his arms. "Darlin', oh, darlin', what happened?" He kissed her forehead as tears trickled down his cheeks.

"It's okay, Papa. I just tripped and fell back in the water. I'm wet, but I'm not hurt really."

Two Bears splashed out and bent down next to the unconscious Tall Owl. He rubbed his smooth chin. "I don't suppose you shot him or stabbed him, Red Bear. I don't see any blood."

Mr. Barre set Retta down on the riverbank. The wet buckskin dress hung heavy on her back. Her moccasins were cold and damp. "He's a very stubborn man. Ansley's horse refuses to be mounted off-side. Tall Owl fell off when the horse's head reared back and crashed into his. All I did was turn him over and prop his head out of the water."

Two Bears examined the Arapaho from head to foot. "Why did you do that?"

Retta put her hands on her hips. "Because I didn't want him to drown—that's why."

Hugh MacGregor strode to the riverbank, Ansley at his side. The others trotted behind them.

"Retta, what did you do to him?" Ansley asked.

"She used an old Shoshone trick," Two Bears replied. "She spooked the horse and let him take care of Tall Owl."

"You did?" Ansley marveled.

"Sort of," Retta replied.

"Looks like we have company." Bobcat pointed across the river as the Cheyenne waded toward them. "The rest of you stay back. Me, Two Bears, and Missy will palaver with them."

Retta squatted on the bank of the river with the two men and waited as the Cheyenne approached. They ignored the unconscious Tall Owl, and the one with the scarred chest spoke to Two Bears.

"What did he say?" Retta whispered to Bouchet.

"He wants to know who to thank for deliverin' that blow to Tall Owl."

Two Bears pointed to Retta.

The three Cheyenne stared at Retta, nodded, and spoke rapidly.

"Are they talking about me?" she quizzed.

Bouchet chewed on the stem of his unlit clay pipe. "Seems they are very impressed with Two Bears's daughter. They want to know your name."

She waited for Two Bears to answer.

Bouchet chuckled.

"What's so funny?" she whispered.

"Two Bears said you were named Red Bear because you have such a pure heart."

"He did?"

The one with the scarred chest delivered a long monologue. When he finished, he pointed for Two Bears to talk to Retta.

The Shoshone scooted over to her and turned his back to the Cheyenne. His voice was low.

"What do they want?" she asked.

"Dance-with-the-Sun, the one with the scars, is the chief's oldest son. He has a younger brother. He wants to know if you will be the young brother's wife."

"What? His wife?"

"That's what he said, Red Bear."

"But—but—I'm only twelve," she stammered.

There was absolutely no emotion in Two Bears's face. "The brother is only fourteen."

Retta felt her throat tighten. She puffed out her cheeks hard and laced her hands on top of her head. "But I'm not even Indian!" she blurted out.

"No, but they think you are," Two Bears replied.

"You ain't serious about this," Bouchet interjected.

Retta scratched in the packed mud at her feet. "I'm not going to marry some chief's son."

Two Bears pointed to the mud. "Yes, that is good. A Shoshone like you should not marry the Cheyenne. But it is an honor to be asked. A refusal must be carefully worded."

Retta peered over Two Bears's shoulder at the Cheyenne men. "Why did they have to ask me? Why don't they just go away?"

"Because they have seen your bravery in action. They are very impressed," Two Bears reported.

"What do you mean?"

"The proof is there in the water. You delivered Tall Owl to them. The Cheyenne do not impress easily. They say you are very courageous for a Shoshone."

"Didn't you explain how it happened?"

"I merely told them they were very wise for Cheyenne." Two Bears drew in the mud. "You will need to give them an answer, Red Bear."

Retta chewed on her lip. *I can stand up and say, "I'm not an Indian." Or I could just run back to Papa. Lord, how come everything I do seems to get me in more and more trouble?*

"Red Bear?" Two Bears prompted.

"Well . . . well . . . tell them . . . tell them they have seen my bravery, but I have not seen the chief's youngest son's bravery; so I won't even consider it. The man I marry must have as brave and pure a heart as mine."

Two Bears turned back around and spoke to the Cheyenne. She could see his dark eyes shine as he spoke. All three men smiled. They seemed to nod their heads in unison as Two Bears explained. Then Dance-with-the-Sun spoke.

Bobcat whispered to her, "He said that you are not only brave but very wise. He's quite impressed. He said if he didn't already have two wives that fight all the time, he would take you for his wife also."

Retta's mouth dropped open. "But—but . . . he's too old!"

Bouchet patted her shoulder. "Don't worry, Missy. He also said that his younger brother was not very brave, and you were correct to answer as you did."

Dance-with-the-Sun pulled a stone hammer from his belt. Rawhide strips bound a big, smooth river rock to the end of a foot-long bone handle. There was a rabbit collar next to the rock, with a short string of beads and a feather dangling down. A rawhide wrist strap hung from the handle. Tiny turquoise and green beads covered the handle's end.

Dance-with-the-Sun shoved the strange object at Retta.

"He wants you to have it," Bouchet whispered.

"Take it and hold it to your heart and look down at the dirt," Two Bears instructed.

She did as she was told.

"What is it?" she murmured.

"I'll tell you later," Bobcat said. "Do like Two Bears said. Keep your eyes down."

The Cheyenne stood. Two Bears motioned for Retta and Bobcat to stand with him. More words were spoken.

Dance-with-the-Sun reached over and put his hand on Retta's shoulder.

"Look up slowly. Do not smile. Nod your head," Two Bears said.

Retta looked into the dark brown eyes of the Cheyenne and nodded her head slowly. *Lord Jesus, help me, because I don't know what I'm doing. I haven't known what I was doing all day. This man has scars inside of him to match those on his chest. I can see it in his eyes.*

The three Cheyenne warriors spun around and walked over to the unconscious Indian. They grabbed Tall Owl's legs and proceeded to drag him across the river, with his head bouncing in and out of the water.

"He could drown," Retta said anxiously.

"I reckon that's the least of his worries." Bobcat put his hand on her shoulder. "You did very good, Missy. You've got more Indian sense than a hundred politicians back in Washington."

"Red Bear is a very smart young lady," Two Bears added. "It is her Shoshone blood."

"But I don't have any Shoshone blood," she grinned. "Or maybe I do."

"What did they want," Ansley called out, "besides that awful Indian?"

"They wanted Missy to marry the chief's son," Bobcat informed her.

"But that can't be!" Ansley gasped, her hands on her hips. "I can't believe this. He asked you to marry someone? I'm thirteen, and no one has ever asked me to marry him."

"Well, it's a good thing!" Mr. MacGregor huffed.

"But—but Retta's only twelve, and—and she's so . . . so . . ."

Retta grinned. "Plain as a pumpkin seed?"

Ansley rolled her eyes. Finally she grinned. "Did I really say that about you?"

"More than once, I believe."

Ansley reached out her hand. Retta hesitated for a moment. Then she reached out and took Ansley's hand.

"Sometimes I do and say things really dumb," Ansley admitted. "Thank you for getting me out of that jam. I was so scared. I really thought I was going to die."

"It just seemed like the right thing to do," Retta murmured.

"I don't know if I would even know the right thing to do," Ansley said. "It's been a long time since I even asked."

"Come on," Bobcat called out. "Let's get our horses. We have a wagon train to catch."

Mr. Barre turned to Two Bears. "You and your family are welcome to join the wagon train. I understand you're going to Fort Bridger."

"I will discuss it with them. If the Cheyenne take Tall Owl and depart, we might just continue to shadow you."

"But you would be welcome with us," Retta called out.

"Some of your friends might not be able to tell a Shoshone from an Arapaho or Cheyenne," Two Bears explained.

Bouchet mounted his horse. "He's got a point there, Missy."

Shy Bear rode over to her. The Indian girl reached down and handed her a leather headband with a feather. Retta retrieved the pansy-plum bonnet and handed it to Shy Bear.

The Indian girl pulled it on her head and grinned. Her waist-length black hair hung down her back. She blurted out one word.

"What did she say? I've never heard her speak before."

"She said, 'sister,'" Bouchet reported.

"Yes, oh yes!" Retta clapped. "And you *are* my sister!"

She watched Two Bears and his family ride south. Then she mounted up behind her father. Retta held the hammer in her right hand and gripped his leather suspenders with her left.

"Darlin', I think that's enough excitement for a while. Perhaps you should stay a little closer to the wagon from now on," Mr. Barre cautioned.

"I prayed that if the Lord would deliver me, I would go to the wagon and hide under the quilt all the way to Oregon."

"Tough to do your chores under there," her father pointed out. "Perhaps you could come out from time to time."

Retta felt the rhythm of the horse beneath her and reached back and patted the chestnut gelding's rump. "I suppose it would be all right if I helped you and Mama out a bit from time to time."

Mr. Barre rubbed his forehead with the palm of his hand as if trying to make the wrinkles disappear. "Everything turned out fine, darlin'. And your sweet mama don't need to hear all the details. It would be a worry to her."

"I can hear Mama now." William grinned as he spurred his horse alongside them. "'Eugene, I will not let my daughter be put in such danger again. Is that understood!'"

Mr. Barre laughed. "That's true, son. I'm convinced that you children have one of the finest mamas God ever created."

"She's been feeling poorly enough lately," Retta commented.

"Yep, but we all know that she'll pull out of it. She always does," Mr. Barre assured them.

"Can I tell Mama about Dance-with-the-Sun asking me to marry his younger brother?"

"I reckon you'll have to, since Ansley will spread that story up and down the train, no matter what you say or don't say."

They rode south of the meandering river, crossed the wagon tracks, and then turned west. Retta studied the distant northern river bluffs. She thought she saw movement, but she couldn't tell if it was the Cheyenne or merely antelope.

"Papa, what's going to happen to Tall Owl?" Retta asked.

Mr. Barre pushed his hat back. "I reckon whatever the Cheyenne think is just and fair."

"Will they torture him? Will they kill him?"

"They might. Every group of people has its own system of punishment. It's called justice."

Retta bit her lip. "I'm worried about him."

"He's a murderer," Mr. Barre stated.

"I know that's what they say, but I never saw him murder anyone. I just feel funny about it."

"Darlin', there are some things we have to leave with the Lord. He likes righteousness to be rewarded and wickedness punished. I reckon He will understand any group of people who aim for that."

"Tall Owl's going to hate me forever."

"Darlin', why don't you pray that Tall Owl will get the exact punishment his crime deserves," her father suggested. "That's what the Lord's justice is all about."

"But grace is getting better than we deserve."

"Yep, that's right."

Retta sat up straight as she bounced along with the horse's gait. "I'll pray that Tall Owl will receive justice *and* grace."

Mr. Barre tugged his wide-brimmed hat down low in

the front. "That's my girl. Would you feel better if we had turned him over to a U.S. marshal, and he had been convicted and hung?"

"Yeah, I would."

"Well, darlin', we did the same thing. This is a different culture. And for a while still, it's their land. So they follow their ways. I reckon old Tall Owl knew what would happen if he were captured."

The brown, grass-covered prairie rose in a swell ahead of them so that they could only see a few hundred yards ahead. The scene was motionless except for their horses and silent except for clopping hooves and muted conversations. Retta noticed the men pull off their hats, and she scanned the trail until she spied four grave markers near the wagon ruts.

"Those are the first graves we've seen since Chimney Rock," she murmured.

"Mr. Bouchet says they'll get thicker as we go further west," William said.

"Remember how we used to stop and cry at the graves? Now we just ride past and tip our hats," she added.

"Only the body gets buried, darlin'. The people are not really there," Mr. Barre explained.

"I know, Papa, but it's still so sad to think that they are buried out here and that their families moved on."

For several moments Retta rode without speaking.

"I hope Mama is feeling better today," she said.

Mr. Barre reached back and patted her shoulder. "Now, baby, I don't want my Shoshone princess to worry too much."

Retta grinned. "You always tell me I'm getting as tan as an Indian."

"Now you believe me."

"I think I brown faster than Mama and Lerryn."

"Those two won't let the sun touch any part of their body."

"I think the boys like girls with pale skin best."

"Only the boys with pale skin. I hear the brown boys find you quite charming."

"Papa! You're teasing me."

"Yes, baby. Don't ever change. You are perfect the way you are."

William rode close and pointed toward Retta's hand. "Tell me about that stone hammer you got, li'l sis."

"It's my present from Dance-with-the-Sun."

"Which one was he?"

"The one with the scars on his chest. Did you see him?"

"Don't reckon I looked them over too close," William admitted. "So what do you do with it? Drive tent pegs?"

"Mr. Bouchet said it's a coup stick," Retta informed him.

"Coo? You mean, like a dove?"

"That's how it sounds, but I don't think it has anything to do with doves."

"It's spelled c - o - u - p. The *p* is silent. So it's pronounced coo," Mr. Barre reported.

Ansley rode back to them. "Retta, do you want to ride with me?"

Retta looked at her in surprise. *Never in my life did Ansley MacGregor want me to ride with her. I wonder what she wants?*

"Please, Retta, I want to talk to you about your Indian friends."

"Papa, can I ride with Ansley? I want to ride up to Mr. Bouchet and ask him about my coup stick. He said he'd explain it to me."

"I reckon so, but that is about as far as I want you out of my sight."

Retta slipped off her father's horse. She reached up and grabbed Ansley's outstretched arm and pulled herself up behind the saddle.

I didn't know Ansley had such strong arms, and yet she smells pretty like Lerryn.

"Just hold on to my waist," Ansley said.

"Your horse is very nice."

"Thanks. He cost fifty dollars, but I probably already told you that."

"I'm going to get a horse soon. A chestnut and white pinto, if I ever find one cheap enough."

"Then we can go riding every day."

"You and me?"

"Sure."

Retta licked her fingers and mashed down her bangs. *Maybe the reason I never get close to Ansley is because I feel so plain and boring around her.*

"Shall we go up and visit with Mr. Bouchet?" Ansley asked.

"Yes," Retta replied. She wrapped her arms around Ansley's narrow waist.

"Mr. Bouchet!" Retta called out as they approached. "You told me you'd explain this coup stick."

"It looks like a stone hammer," Ansley said. "Can I see it, Retta?"

Retta handed it to her.

Bobcat spurred his horse to a slow trot. His dirty hat slipped to his back, held around his neck by a stampede string. "Ladies, that there is an Indian hammer for tappin' on heads."

"They use it for a weapon?" Retta asked.

"Missy, the Indians use a stick like that to measure bravery. When you get close enough to an enemy to tap him with that stone hammer, they claim you can 'count coup.'"

"You mean, kill someone with it?" Retta questioned.

"Not necessarily. Just tappin' the person is enough to prove how courageous you are. If you can get that close to your enemy and come away alive, you are considered a very brave warrior. Course, I'd imagine ol' Dance-with-the-Sun has bashed in a skull or two in his day with that coup stick."

Ansley immediately handed the stick back to Retta and rubbed the palms of her hands on her skirt.

Retta stroked the soft rabbit fur near the rock. "But why did he give it to me?"

Bobcat stood in the stirrups and gazed at the rising prairie in the west. Retta followed his gaze but didn't see anything. He plopped back down. "Because you 'counted coup' with Tall Owl. You got close enough to touch him."

"I got close enough to touch him, too," Ansley asserted.

"Well, Miss MacGregor," Bobcat replied, "being captured and tied up don't exactly count as an act of bravery."

"The Lord answered our prayer. That's why it turned out like it did," Retta said.

"You might have gotten a bigger answer than you think. That coup stick in your hand is mighty special. It has Dance-with-the-Sun's mark on it. He said that Retta could ride into any Cheyenne or Sioux camp on the plains and be accepted when she carries that coup stick."

"Really?" Retta squealed.

"It's kind of like a free pass, I reckon. As long as you wear that buckskin dress and carry the coup stick, you'll be safe. He said he'll send word from band to band about Red Bear of the Shoshone and how brave she was." Again Bouchet stood in the stirrups. "Looks like the whole train up there."

"There's the California bunch!" Retta called out. "Papa, can we ride ahead and see Joslyn?"

"I reckon so, but check in with Mama first. I don't want her to fret over you anymore."

Retta and Ansley galloped up to the column of parked wagons. The Oregon-bound wagons were parked in a long line to the north of the main trail. Many of the California-bound ones were sunk to the axles in mud. Men shouted instructions as the oxen strained and heaved to tug the wagons out of the bog.

Ansley let Retta off at her wagon and then rode on up the line. Lerryn's head poked out the yellow flap at the back of the Barre wagon. "It's about time you got back," she shouted. "Where's Papa?"

Retta gazed over her shoulder. "He's back at the Neilsen wagon."

"Go get him quick. Mama's real sick. She's crying and mumbling and saying it might be her time!"

Seven

Retta huddled at one end of the covered wagon and slipped off her wet buckskin dress and moccasins. She yanked her green calico dress out of the small trunk and eased it over her head. Her mother was stretched out over quilts at the far end of the wagon. She watched the back of her father's head as he leaned over and toweled perspiration off his wife's face.

"Eugene, I told you this would happen," Mrs. Barre said.

"I know, darlin'. You were right. I let the Donation Land Act blind me, I suppose. I can't believe I'm doin' this for 320 acres in Oregon."

"And 320 acres for me," she added.

"Still it's foolishness that drives a man to take such chances. I always figured I was smarter than this."

"It's not your fault, Eugene. You need a stronger woman than me."

"Julia Carter Barre, you are all I ever needed in my life. You know that."

"And Oregon."

"What?"

"You need Oregon, too, don't you?"

"Right now, I just need you. It doesn't matter if we're in

Oregon, Ohio, Nebraska, or wherever it is we are today. So hang on for me," he urged.

Mrs. Barre's voice sounded weak, pained. "I wanted to be strong for you."

"You just need some rest. Relax now. Me and the kids will take care of things."

"No, I can't let you down. I need to cook."

Retta brushed down the front of her dress and tied the ribbon belt behind her. "I can cook, Mama," she offered.

"Oh, Coretta Emily, I didn't see you back there."

"I was changing my dress."

"Did you get your buckskin dirty?"

"I got it wet, and it's heavy."

"I imagine it is."

"Mama, I really can cook for you. I can boil potatoes and make gravy. Grandma Cutler taught me how to do gravy last November."

"Come here, Coretta."

Retta crawled up next to her father. "Mama, you've been crying."

"Yes, darlin', I've been hurting so bad I cried."

"Why, Mama? What's wrong? Isn't there any medicine you can take? That man in Independence had some Female Remedy. Remember? Couldn't you take that?"

Her mother reached out her hand. Retta grabbed her fingers. "Mama, your hand is cold and sweaty at the same time."

"I know, baby. I can't decide whether to have a chill or a fever."

Retta studied her mother's face. "Mama, you don't look so good."

"Now, darlin', I think your mama is beautiful," Mr. Barre maintained.

"Eugene, our Retta is the most honest girl on the face of the earth. When she says I look horrid, then I look horrid."

"Oh no, Mama, I didn't mean horrid. I meant sickly, peaked, anemic, tired, and run-down, but I didn't mean horrid!"

Mrs. Barre forced a smile. "Thank you for that explanation."

"You're welcome."

Her mother's squeeze was feeble. "Where's your sister?"

The voice filtered in from outside the back flap. "I'm out here, Mama."

"Me and Andrew are out here, too, Mama," William called.

"My, I have taken all of you from your chores."

"They aren't as important as you," Andrew replied.

"I'm as good as I can be right now, as long as the wagon doesn't have to move. So you men go on and help pull those wagons out of the mud."

"Not until you're better, Julia darlin'," Mr. Barre said.

"Now, Eugene, we both know I might not get better ever. So you go on. I'll have my girls to look after me," she replied.

He didn't budge.

"There isn't anything you can do that Lerryn and Coretta can't do."

Mr. Barre stood to leave. Even though he had to stoop in the wagon, he towered above Retta. He motioned for her to climb down out of the wagon with him. As they did, Lerryn scurried back in.

Her father led Retta a little ways away. "Darlin', your mama is very sick. Most of it is my fault. I should never have brought her out here. At the least, I should have waited until next year. But I was too set on gettin' to Oregon and gettin' that 640 acres. Now your mama has to pay for my impatience. I need you and your sis to take good care of her."

"We will, Papa."

"And come get me the minute she needs anything you can't handle."

Retta laced her fingers together and rested them on top of her head. "I will, Papa. I'll come find you."

Mr. Barre started to walk away, then paused, and turned back. "Darlin', I'm very proud of what you did today with that Arapaho."

"I was just trying to do what was right, Papa."

"You did well, Coretta. Your mama did a good job of raisin' you."

"You raised me, too, Papa."

He stared at her for several moments and then nodded. "Yep, you're right. That's probably why you get into so many scrapes."

"I'm going to try real hard from now on to stay out of trouble."

"Baby, that's okay. You keep right on havin' a good time. You'll have your share of tough times. Everybody does. Okay, the boys and I will be helpin' Mr. Landers pull his wagon out of the bog. We aren't goin' to move before mornin'. You go ahead and build a fire if you want to."

Retta crawled back up in the wagon. Lerryn now sat next to Mrs. Barre. She held her fingers up to her lips. "Mama's sleepin', Retta. I'll sit with her."

"What do you want me to do? Can I cook supper?"

"I think it's too early for supper."

"Can I make a dessert?" Retta asked her sister.

"Okay, but try not to make too much noise."

Retta's fire was burning well when Ben Weaver and Travis Lott trotted up.

"Hi, Retta! Is it true you're going to marry an Indian chief someday?" Ben blurted out.

"No! Who told you that?"

"Ansley said that you told the Indians that if the chief's son did a brave act, you would consider marrying him," Travis replied.

With her chin on her chest, Retta mumbled, "I never said I was going to consider marrying anyone. I was told that he's not very brave."

Ben's hair curled out from under his hat "But he did want you to marry him?"

Retta dug through a big blue box labeled "Food." "Yeah, well, sort of," she replied.

"And you captured that Indian named Tall Owl?" Ben pressed.

"The horse bucked him off, and he hit his head."

"How come you have all the adventures?" Travis sputtered.

"It all happened so fast I hardly got to enjoy it." Retta pulled out a small burlap sack.

"And Mr. Bouchet said they gave you a spear or somethin' that will let you go into a Cheyenne camp any time you want and not get scalped," Ben said.

"It's a coup stick, not a spear."

Ben peeked into the blue box. "I can't believe how ever'thing happens to you. Is that some raisins?"

"Yes, and you may not have any." She closed the lid on the box. "Before the last couple of days, everything was pretty routine. You told me I was boring."

Ben scratched his neck. "I might have been a tad premature with that judgment."

"What're you goin' to do now, Retta?" Travis asked.

"Crack walnuts," she replied.

"What?"

"I'm making walnut-raisin pudding, and so I need to crack walnuts. Isn't that an exciting adventure?"

"Eh, not really, but I'm goin' to stay here anyway." Ben turned to Travis. "I'll take the first watch."

Retta's eyes bored into Ben's. "What do you mean, the first watch?"

Ben shifted his weight from one foot to the other. "Me and Travis decided that the only way we could get in on your adventures is to have one of us stationed with you at all times."

"All times? Even at night?"

"No, not at night," Travis replied. "You do go to sleep, don't you?"

Retta hustled to the brown crate labeled "Dishes" and pulled out a white-enameled tin bowl. "Yes, I do, but what if I don't want you hanging around?"

"Why not?" Ben scooted closer and lowered his voice. "Do you have another adventure planned that you don't want to tell us about?"

"I never plan adventures," she said. "They just happen."

"See? That's exactly why one of us has to stay with you," Ben declared.

"Then you might as well help me." Retta motioned toward the wagon. "Fetch me that keg of nails."

"What're you goin' to build?"

"I'm going to use it as a bench to crack walnuts on."

Ben staggered as he carried the keg of nails over to Retta.

"Now pull Mama's dish crate over here. We'll use it for a chair."

"W-we?" Ben stammered as he dragged the heavy crate.

"You didn't reckon on sitting around staring at me

and saying nothing like you do when you go see Ansley, did you?"

Ben blushed strawberry red. "Trav . . . help me with this crate."

"I'll get the nutcracker." Retta climbed up in the wagon and spied both Lerryn and her mother asleep. She grabbed up her coup stick. When she came back to the fire, Ben was perched on one end of the brown crate. She carried the small burlap bag over to the nail keg.

"Where's Travis?"

"He said I have the first shift. What do you have in your hand?" Ben asked.

"Oh," she grinned, "this is a sack of walnuts from our tree in Ohio."

"No, in the other hand."

"Oh, this?" She held the coup stick up as if to strike him.

Ben jumped back. "Yeah, did you get that from the Shoshone?"

"No, I got it from Dance-with-the-Sun. He's Cheyenne. It's a coup stick, for 'counting coup.' Of course, you know all about that."

"Eh," Ben stammered, "sure, but what're you goin' to use it for?"

"Cracking walnuts."

"How does that work?"

"You hold the walnut on top of the nail keg with two fingers. I'll smash it with this. Then we pick out the meat."

"Smash it? But—but what if you hit my fingers?" he protested.

Retta laughed. "Then that will be quite an adventure, won't it, Ben Weaver?"

After supper Mr. Barre left to talk with Colonel Graves and

Bobcat Bouchet. Andrew took the first shift at night watch over the horses. William wandered up the wagon train to visit Amy Lynch. Lerryn went back in the wagon to stay with Mrs. Barre.

Retta washed dishes.

Ben dried them.

And Travis played with the coup stick. "This sucker is heavy. I bet it would hurt to get hit with it. Retta, do you really think the one who carries this will be safe in a Cheyenne camp?"

"Yes, provided the person wears a buckskin dress."

Travis swallowed hard. "A dress?"

"Well, Dance-with-the-Sun said he would tell the story about the Indian girl who was so brave."

"You don't look like an Indian," Travis insisted.

"Oh, I don't know. Retta's got dark brown, thick hair," Ben interjected.

"So do lots of girls, but that don't make them Indians."

"And she has a round nose," Ben countered.

"So do I," Travis retorted. "That don't mean nothin'."

"That's 'cause you broke yours when you got bucked off your horse."

"I didn't get bucked off," Travis argued. "Samson stepped in a prairie dog hole, that's what. I say Retta don't look like no Indian."

"She's got strong arms and shoulders. Did you ever get punched by her?" Ben argued.

"No, but strong arms don't make her look like an Indian."

"The Shoshone, Arapaho, and Cheyenne think she does."

"What do they know?" Travis shrugged.

"I reckon they know what an Indian girl's body looks like."

Retta hid her face behind the wet dishrag. "You two are embarrassing me. Stop it right now!"

"Maybe you're right, Ben," Travis laughed. "I do see some red in her face and neck."

"Give me my coup stick!" Retta yanked the stone hammer from Travis's hand. "The next word either of you say about how I look, I'm going to demonstrate what it feels like to be struck in the back of the head with a coup stick."

"Hi, Retta!" The voice was light, feminine.

She glanced up to see Joslyn, black hair bouncing in the evening shadows. "Hi, River Raven."

"Are you having a party?" Joslyn asked.

"Oh, yes. A dishwashing party. You want to join us?"

"No, I just had one of those. You know what? Mr. Landers said we aren't going to break off and go to California. He said we really need to stay with the train, at least until Fort Hall."

"Oh, that's wonderful. It's an answer to my prayer."

"Do you pray a lot, Retta?" Travis asked.

"Only when I'm scared or lonely or worried or angry or happy or tired or feeling really, really good," she said.

"Did you know that Gilson hasn't left her wagon now for two days?" Joslyn reported.

"Oh, we must go see her," Retta declared.

"She might be asleep."

"Let's go right now. Ben and Travis can finish the dishes."

"What? We're goin' with you," Ben insisted.

"We're going to visit a sick friend. It will not be an adventure," Retta stated.

"It could be if Gilson vomits again," Joslyn quipped.

"Eh, if we stay here, can we look at your coup stick?" Travis asked.

"Sure, but don't go carrying it off anywhere."

"How about that eagle-feather headband? Can we look at it too?" Travis asked.

Retta opened the dark green cloth valise and pulled out the headband. "But you have to finish the dishes first."

Ben dried his hands on the towel and picked up the headband. "You promise you won't have any adventures?"

"It will just be dull girl chat."

"*You* aren't dull anymore, Retta," Ben remarked.

"Oh, thanks." Joslyn scowled. "I take that to mean *I'm* boring."

"Oh, no," Ben assured her. "Individual girls aren't tiresome. It's when you all get together that it gets wearisome."

"Thank you," Retta giggled. "I'm glad you explained that."

Ben shoved the headband down on his bushy blond hair. "You're welcome."

By the time Retta and Joslyn reached the O'Day wagon, Christen Weaver had joined them. Retta led the procession. "Hi, Mrs. O'Day. We came to visit Gilson."

The tall woman brushed a wisp of gray hair from her eye. "Retta Barre, what is all this I hear about you?"

Retta rocked back on her heels. "You mean, with the Indians?"

"My dear girl, I hear that you might be the most daring young lady to head down the Oregon Trail."

Retta dropped her head to her chest. "I think it's just 'cause I get into more trouble, and the Lord is gracious to rescue me."

Mrs. O'Day wiped her large hands on her apron. "But how did you know what to do when you were alone with those savages?"

"I guess I forgot they were savages and just thought of them as people, and I, eh, prayed a lot."

Mrs. O'Day stared at Retta for a minute and then looked up at her wagon. "That's good, darlin'. You keep prayin' for as long as you can. The day may come when you can't pray anymore. I ran out of prayers years ago."

"You can't run out of prayers!" Christen exclaimed.

"You girls are young yet. You'll learn someday, I reckon. I prayed for over ten years for the Lord to heal my Gilson. I don't reckon I should keep pesterin' Him since He seems to want her sick."

"Since I haven't run out of prayers, Mrs. O'Day, may I continue to pray for Gilson?" Retta asked.

Mrs. O'Day moved several feet away from the wagon and stared out into the twilight on the prairie. "Yeah . . . you do that, darlin'."

"May we go see Gilson now?" Joslyn asked.

Mrs. O'Day untied her apron. "Would you girls stay with her a few minutes? I need to . . . get some fresh air."

"Sure." Retta nodded.

They watched Mrs. O'Day stroll out into the short buffalo grass lapping along the North Platte River Valley.

"What did she mean, fresh air?" Christen asked. "We're outside."

"Maybe she just needs to be alone. I don't think she's feeling too good either," Retta offered.

Joslyn climbed up first. She yanked back the flap as the other two clambered up behind her. "Put on your robe, Gilson. You have company!" Joslyn called out.

Retta scooted into the wagon. "Where is she?"

"She's gone!" Joslyn declared.

"Gone?" Christen said. "She's too sick to go any-where."

"Well, she's not here," Joslyn maintained.

Retta turned up the wick on the small oil lamp. "Her

mama thinks she's here." She stuck her head out of the opening at the front of the wagon. "Mrs. O'Day?" she called.

There was no answer.

"Retta!" Christen cried. "Retta, come here!"

Retta could feel the hair on her arms prickle as she spun around. "What is it?"

"A note!" Joslyn exclaimed. "She's given up, Retta. Gilson's given up."

Joslyn shoved an envelope at Retta. There was writing on the back of it. Retta held it up to the dim lamp.

Dearest Mama,

I just can't do it anymore. I'm so tired. I hurt all over. I'm not strong like Retta, Mama. I'm so scared all the time. I'm afraid of living. I'm afraid of dying. You and Papa go to Oregon and start that farm. I know I will be buried along the trail like all the others. I've known that since we left Missouri. But maybe you could put a marker in Oregon for me. I wanted to make it, Mama. I really did. I love you and Papa. But I'm so tired of living, and you're tired of praying. So good-bye, Mama and Papa.

Your daughter, Gilson Corrine O'Day.

Eight

Retta folded her arms across her chest and forced the tears back. "We're going to find her."

Christen peered out the back of the O'Day wagon. "It's getting quite dark."

Retta folded the envelope with Gilson's note and stuffed it into her dress sleeve. "She's not that strong. She can't be far."

Joslyn picked up a small tintype picture of Gilson that lay on top of a crate. "Why would she want to run off in the dark?"

Retta peeked out the back of the wagon. "You're right. It's pitch-black out there."

"But her parents love her so much." Joslyn laid the tintype back on the crate. "It's dumb to run off."

Christen wrinkled her nose. "Couldn't we just stand beside the wagon and yell for her?"

"No, that will alarm everyone." Retta closed the wagon flap and sat on the edge of a water keg. "We have to find her and bring her back before her mother even knows she's gone."

"How are we going to do that?" Christen asked.

Retta rested her elbows on her knees, her chin on her hand. The air in the wagon was musty and reeked of menthol salve. "If you were really depressed and didn't want to keep on living, where would you go?"

"I wouldn't wander out on the dark prairie at night!" Christen declared. "Why, the Indians might get me . . . or wild animals . . . or outlaws . . . or . . . Oh, well, if I didn't want to live, maybe I would just walk out on the prairie."

"But I wouldn't go toward the river," Joslyn added.

"Why?" Retta questioned.

"Because the water is too shallow to drown in, at least nearby, and the men graze the cattle and horses that way and would find me."

Retta reached down to the quilts and plucked up a small porcelain-headed doll. "In that case, I think I would just walk south."

"Where?" Christen asked. "There's nothing to the south."

"That's exactly why I would go there." Retta stroked the dark-haired doll. "If I felt like Gilson, I would walk and walk and walk and walk until I got tired or fell down, and then . . . then I'd just sleep in the grass and hope I never woke up."

"You would?" Christen gasped.

Retta carefully tucked the doll under the quilt. Its head rested on the tattered pillowcase. "If I hurt bad and was as melancholy as Gilson, I would."

Joslyn stuck her head out the back of the wagon and then pulled it back in. "But how're we going to find her without getting lost ourselves?"

Retta chewed her lip. She glanced around the wagon. Her gaze fixed on the lamp. "Let's each take a candle. We can hike south until we can barely see the wagon train, and then one of us could be posted there. The other two will hike farther south until we can barely see that first candle. Then the second sentinel will be posted, and the last one will go out to where she can barely see the last candle."

"And then what?" Joslyn asked.

Retta folded her hands beneath her chin as if to pray. "We'll call and call for Gilson."

"And if we don't find her?" Christen posed the question.

Retta dropped her hands to her side. "We'll . . . we'll come back here and report it all to Mrs. O'Day. It will only take a little while. We've got to try."

Christen picked up the small wagon lamp. "You mean, we'll just stand out there on the prairie and hold a candle all by ourselves?"

Retta stood and brushed her bangs out of her eyes. "Yes, but not for very long."

"In the dark?" Christen whimpered.

"You'll have candlelight." Retta licked her fingers and tried to smooth down her thick hair.

"Will we carry guns?" Joslyn asked.

Retta glanced at Joslyn's shiny black hair all in place. "Do you have a gun?"

Joslyn's narrow nose wiggled in a grimace. "Eh, no."

Retta scooted past the girls to the front of the O'Day wagon. "It won't be too bad. We'll be able to see each other's candles at all times."

Joslyn slipped her hand into Retta's and asked in a soft voice, "Do you really think we can find Gilson?"

Retta squeezed her fingers. "We'll probably find her by the second candle."

"I've got those fat candles we made for the church bazaar back in Ohio," Christen offered. "I was saving them for a real emergency."

"This is a real emergency. How many do you have?" Retta asked.

"Six."

"Bring them all," Retta urged. "We'll have two each." She climbed out of the wagon and waited for the other two.

"I'm barefoot. I need to get my shoes," Joslyn said.

"Hurry," Retta directed.

"I'll do it . . . only if . . ." Christen paused.

"If what?" Joslyn asked.

"If Retta wears her buckskins and brings her coup stick with us just in case," Christen blurted out.

Retta put her hands on her hips. "We're only going to be a few hundred yards from the wagon train. We must hurry."

"Please, Retta," Christen begged.

"Okay . . . we'll meet back here."

"What if Mrs. O'Day returns?" Joslyn asked.

"We'll tell her the truth," Retta replied.

Christen pointed to the envelope up her sleeve. "And show her that note?"

"Oh, the note." Retta bit her lip and felt for the folded envelope. *Lord Jesus, I really don't want Mrs. O'Day to be hurt by this note.* "Let's just pray we can get Gilson back before she's missed."

When Retta reached her wagon, Ben and Travis lounged on the green trunk next to the lamp. Travis waved the coup stick. Ben wore the eagle-feather headband.

"Did you have any adventures without us?" Ben asked.

"Eh, nope. Did you?"

"Shoot, we jist now got done with them dishes." Travis pointed to the basin full of water.

She reached out her hand. "Travis, I need that coup stick."

He handed the rock hammer to her, and both boys jumped up. "How come, Retta? Are you goin' after Indians again?"

She looked away from the boys. "No, of course not."

Ben scooted around in front of her. "Then what're you doin'?"

Retta glanced down at the packed dirt next to the wagon wheel. "Christen wanted me to bring it. Gilson hasn't seen it yet."

Ben tugged on his leather suspenders. "Maybe we'll just come with you."

Retta shook her head. "No reason for that."

Travis sidled up next to Ben. "You don't want us to come?"

"You can come, but you can't go into Gilson's wagon."

"Why?" Ben pressed.

"There's not enough room. Besides, she could be sleeping," Retta replied.

Travis leaned real close to Retta. "You're plannin' to show a coup stick to someone who's asleep?"

Ben scooted close to the other side of her. "Sounds like an adventure cookin' to me."

"So we'll just tag along," Travis declared.

Ben shoved his hands in the front pockets of his ducking trousers. "You don't mind if I wear this headband awhile, do you?"

Retta giggled at the feather hanging down over Ben's ear. "No, I don't mind. As long as you don't mind."

"What do you mean by that?"

"Mr. Bouchet says that a single feather swooping to the front like that with those colored beads means the wearer is an unmarried girl . . . in case someone's looking for a wife."

Travis hooted.

Retta giggled some more.

Ben jerked the headband off and tossed it to her. "I reckon I'll wear my hat. Did he really say that?"

Retta put the headband back into the valise. "Actually no. I just made it up to watch you squirm. But it might mean that. Wouldn't you like to know what it means before you wear it?"

"Yeah, I reckon," Ben mumbled. "But we're still goin' with you to Gilson's."

"Have you got any sulfur matches?" she asked.

"Yeah, I've got three," Ben reported. "Why?"

Retta raised her round nose and blinked her eyelids. "You certainly can't have much of an adventure on the prairie if it's pitch-black."

"I knew it!" Ben yelped. "You've got something stirrin'. Where do we meet?"

"At Gilson's."

"Is this a scavenger hunt, Retta?" Travis asked.

"Sort of."

Ben followed her toward the front of the wagon. "What're we lookin' for?"

Retta swung the coup stick in a circle. "Gilson."

As Ben and Travis trotted away, Retta crawled up into the wagon. Two people sat next to her sleeping mother.

"Andrew? . . . Oh . . ."

Her sister glared at her.

"Hi, Brian. I thought you were my brother."

"Brian came to sit with me. Isn't that nice?" Lerryn said in her prim and proper voice.

"Yeah . . . I think so."

Lerryn folded her hands across her chest and tilted her head. "What do you want?"

Retta looked down at the front of her own dress. "I just wanted to know if Mama is okay." *Lerryn has beautiful fingers. She has beautiful everything.*

"She woke up, and we visited for a while. Then she took some water and went back to sleep."

"I reckon that's good for her." Retta inched a little closer to her mother. "I wonder if you hurt as bad when you're asleep?"

"Maybe the body still hurts, but the mind doesn't," Brian offered.

She scooted a little closer. "Yeah, I reckon."

"Retta, I'll watch Mama for a while longer. You go play with your friends if you want to." Lerryn dismissed her with a sweep of her hand.

Retta started to the front of the wagon and then turned back. "But who will go fetch Papa if Mama wakes up in bad straits?"

"I will," Brian volunteered.

"I'll be up by Gilson's if you need me."

"Bye, Retta," Lerryn said.

"Bye."

She climbed back down, snatched up her coup stick, and trotted along the line of dimly lit wagons.

"Retta!"

She stopped running when she heard the voice.

"William?"

There was a giggle in the shadows.

"Eh . . . Amy is here with me," her brother admitted.

"Yeah, so I noticed."

"Hi, Retta."

"Hi, Amy."

"Is Mama still sleepin'?" William asked.

"Yes. You know how tired she's been. It's good for her." Amy's arm was tucked into her brother's.

"Is big sis with her?" he asked.

Retta watched her brother. "Yes, and Brian is there, too." *The problem with having handsome brothers is that it makes all the other boys look so plain.*

"Maybe me and Amy can go spell them off," William offered.

Retta glanced back down the row of wagons. "That would be nice. . . . Eh . . . I'm sure they will be pleased to see you." *I know, Lord, I know. Lerryn will hate me for it, but I'm doing this for her own good.*

"Where are you headed?" William asked her.

Retta pointed up the line of wagons. "I'll be up by Gilson O'Day's."

"What's the coup stick for?" he challenged.

"We're going on something like a scavenger hunt."

"Go on, little sis, and play." He turned to Amy. "When you're young, every day is an adventure."

"William Henry Barre," Amy purred, "are you telling me you're too old for an adventure?"

Retta rolled her eyes and trotted up the line.

When she got to Gilson's wagon, Christen waited with Ben and Travis. "They said you invited them," she said.

"They invited themselves," Retta said, "but I figure the more people we have, the deeper into the prairie we can go."

"You didn't wear your buckskin dress."

"There was no place to change. Brian is helping Lerryn watch Mama."

"And who is watching them?"

"William and Amy will be real soon." Retta stared out into the dark. "Where's Joslyn?"

Christen pointed to the shadows behind her. "Here she comes . . . with Ansley!"

Retta turned to see two girls in long dresses trot toward them.

"Were you going to do something fun and not invite me, Coretta Barre?" Ansley called out.

Retta huddled them all together. "It's not exactly a fun

excursion, Ansley, but I'm glad you're here. We can use the help."

"What's this all about?" Ansley smiled. "Whose team am I on? I'll be with Ben and Travis."

"We're all on Gilson's team," Retta replied.

After explaining the situation, Retta led them out into the darkness of the prairie carrying their candles. When they reached the point where the wagon lights dimmed in the distance, she halted them near a sand berm. "This is Christen's post," she announced.

"For which I'm very glad," Christen replied. "This is about as far away from the wagons as I want to be."

They left Christen and hiked farther into the darkness.

"Gilson?" Retta called out. "Can you hear me? We've come to find you."

"Don't you reckon she's out farther than this?" Travis asked.

"I suppose."

"Who's next to be stationed?" Ansley asked.

"Ask Retta. She's the leader of this troop," Ben replied.

Lord, it's funny. I've never been the leader of anything before. Especially when it comes to boys . . . and girls like Ansley! I don't even know if I know how to lead. She waved her coup stick like a teacher's pointer. "Well . . . let's have, um, Travis next, then Joslyn, then Ben, then Ansley, and I'll be last."

"Why am I way out there?" Ansley protested.

"Because you're the only one who carries a gun." Retta shrugged.

"Here, take the gun. I don't want it. I'll stand between Travis and Ben," Ansley insisted.

"I'll take the gun," Joslyn offered. "And I'll go way out with Retta."

"But you'll stand wherever Retta tells you to stand," Travis declared.

Retta led them farther into the darkness. "That's fine, Ansley. You can stand between the boys. Maybe we'll find her before we get clear out there anyway."

When Retta stopped, they all stopped. She called into the darkness, "Gilson! Gilson, it's me—Retta. Where are you?"

The night sky had lost all tints of gray and had turned a deep black. Stars flickered above the prairie. The wind drifted from the northwest. They shielded their candle flames with their bodies.

Lord, I'm sort of glad we didn't find her real quick because I don't know what to say to her yet. I've never been sick all the time like Gilson. So I guess I don't really know how she feels. But I know You love her, and You must have more for her to do than just die alone out on the prairie.

So if You could lead us to her and tell me something wise to say to convince her to come back, I'd appreciate it. I just know it isn't Your will that she die out here.

Retta's eyes searched the knee-high prairie grass that parted as she waded through it.

"I'd better stay here, Retta," Travis called.

"Okay, we'll go on," she said. "Gilson, where are you? Answer me, please. If you hear me, please answer."

She could feel the prairie start to slope downward. As it did, the grass waved taller.

"I'll need to stay up here on this crest, or I won't see Travis's candle," Ansley told her.

"Okay. We'll go a little farther."

"Gilson! Gilson!" Joslyn called.

"Gilson, this is Ben. Can you hear me?"

Retta tramped ahead of the other two. *Lord, I guess I really don't know what Your will is for Gilson. I don't even know what it is for me. But I really like Gilson, and she wants to see Oregon, and she's only twelve, so I'm praying she will.*

"You see anything, Retta?" Ben asked.

Retta looked around. "Nothing but prairie grass. It just goes on and on, doesn't it?"

"I bet a man could raise a bunch of beef cows out here," Ben commented. "I still don't know why ever'one wants to go clean to Oregon. This might be good land out here."

"My stepdaddy says there's a war comin' over the slaves, and he wants to be as far away from it as possible," Joslyn said.

Retta continued to stare out into the darkness. "We just got through with that war down in Mexico. Papa said Christian charity would rule, and the Southerners would change after the next election."

"He's a dreamer," Ben said. "I say even the Missouri Compromise is just a stall. The fact remains, the cows would surely like this country. Ain't nothin' to eat the grass out here except buffalo."

"Gilson!" Retta shouted.

"Oh, my," Joslyn cried, "here we are, deep in the prairie. What if we get run over by ten thousand buffalo?"

"Gilson! It's Retta and Ben and Joslyn. Where are you?"

"If there were lots of buffalo around, the ground would start rumbling," Joslyn added.

Ben stomped on the ground. "Like this!"

"Very funny! When the buffalo charge, at least I'll have a gun," Joslyn commented.

"What good would that do you?" he laughed. "That little pistol wouldn't stop a buffalo."

"No, but I could shoot myself so I wouldn't get trampled to death," Joslyn declared. "I read in a penny-press novel about a girl who was prepared to do that."

"But she didn't have to do it?"

"Her horse saved her."

"Ben, you stay here," Retta ordered.

"Yes, ma'am."

Retta glanced at Joslyn and grinned. *No one in my life ever said "yes, ma'am" to me before.* "Come on, Joslyn, there are no buffalo out here."

Joslyn trudged alongside Retta, her long, straight black hair partially dangling over her eyes. "There's no Gilson either."

They hiked another two hundred feet and paused.

"Gilson? Can you hear me? It's Retta and Joslyn. Please answer if you can! Gilson!"

Both girls paused to listen.

"Do you hear anything?" Joslyn asked.

Retta held her candle above her head and leaned forward.

"No. Do you?"

Joslyn's voice was shaky, high-pitched. "I thought I heard a bear snort."

Nine

Retta's eyes searched the horizon in the black prairie night. "A bear? In the middle of the plains?"

Joslyn threw her shoulders back. "I thought I heard a bear snort. There are bears at my grandma's house in Michigan. I know what a bear sounds like." Joslyn cocked the hammer back on the pistol.

Retta glanced back at her. "What're you doing?"

Wide-eyed, Joslyn pointed the pistol out into the night. "I'm getting ready to shoot the bear."

Retta touched her arm with the coup stick. "There's no bear."

"There might be one. Maybe it's lost."

"Joslyn, give me the gun." Retta held out her hand.

"Why?"

"Because I'm afraid I'll be the one to get shot."

Joslyn let the hammer down on the revolver. "Okay. I won't shoot."

"Promise?"

"Unless I see a bear."

"I'm going down this slope until your candle looks dim. Then I'm going to search around. We will probably have to hike back to the wagon train and tell Mrs. O'Day about Gilson. I guess this was not a very good plan."

"But at least it was a plan, Retta. None of the rest of us can even think of a plan."

"You wait there, Joslyn, and don't shoot anyone."

"I'll wait. If you see a bear, holler 'bear.'"

Retta trudged down into the darkness. The prairie grass thickened and felt prickly when it brushed against her. She held her stubby, round candle in front of her. Its puny flame illuminated one step at a time.

Lord, how come some plans seem so good when I'm making them, but they don't turn out to be much when I actually do them? Maybe Gilson went another direction. Maybe she doesn't want us to find her. Maybe she's already . . . oh . . . I think . . . I think I'd better go back soon. The farther I get from the wagon train, the more wild thoughts I get.

Retta glanced back. She could barely see the tiny flicker of Joslyn's candle. She cleared her throat. "Gilson? Gilson, are you there? Please call out to me. This is Retta. Where are you?"

Okay, Lord, I tried. I'm not real smart sometimes, but I tried my best. And now . . . well, it's all in Your hands, Lord.

At the exact moment Retta turned back to look for Joslyn's candle, she heard a soft, deep snort.

The bear!

She spun back around, the candle out in front of her, her coup stick raised. She could see nothing.

"I heard you. I know you're there. I have a coup stick. Don't you come near me," she hollered.

Silence.

She backed up toward Joslyn.

Another snort.

Again she spun around. She saw nothing but the prairie grass directly in front of her.

"Don't you sneak up on me!" she warned. She took two steps into the tall grass. The snort sounded closer.

And lower.

"Are you in this grass? Well, I don't think it's very nice of you to crouch down in the grass and pounce on innocent girls who are merely looking for a sick friend. Oh, you better not have hurt my friend Gilson, or else you are in big trouble!"

The grass moved.

A massive dark head reared up.

Forelegs raised.

It IS a bear!

The hind legs came up.

No. It has four legs like a . . . It's a buffalo! Oh no! We stumbled into a herd of buffalo. They'll trample us to death.

The buffalo staggered and dropped back down on its rear haunches.

Retta's voice quivered. "What's the matter?"

The buffalo snorted.

Retta crept around to the side of the buffalo, holding the candle above her head.

"You've been shot. Oh, poor thing. You can't go any farther, can you? You are just like Gilson, wounded and weak. May the Lord have mercy on you, Mr. Buffalo. He knows where the sparrows are, so I reckon He knows where you are, too."

Retta puffed out her cheeks and held the candle high above the buffalo's head and looked around.

"Are you all alone? Did the others go on without you? This is your prairie. All buffalo die sooner or later out here. But you see, I must find Gilson because she's not a buffalo, and I think she should have something better. So good-bye, Mr. Buffalo."

Retta spun back around and started to hike toward Joslyn. She had made it about halfway when she heard another snort. She turned around and held up her candle. The massive buffalo limped along behind her.

"What're you doing back there? I can't help you. You simply must go back to . . . well, to wherever buffaloes go."

"Retta," Joslyn yelled, "who're you talking to? Did you find Gilson?"

Retta rested the coup stick on her shoulder. "No, I didn't find her. I'm talking to this buffalo."

"You're talking to what?" Joslyn croaked.

"Oh, there's a wounded buffalo back here. It keeps following me. I've told it to go home."

She could hear Joslyn pant and gasp. "A real buffalo?"

Retta stopped when she reached Joslyn. "Yes, and he's such a nuisance."

"Ah . . ah," Joslyn stammered as she stared over Retta's shoulder. "It *is* a real buffalo!"

Retta shrugged and marched on up the prairie slope. "I think that's the only kind there are."

Joslyn's hand shook as it held the revolver. "Shall I shoot it?"

Retta took her arm and led Joslyn along. "No. The poor thing has been shot already. That's why he's limping."

"What're you going to do with him?"

"Nothing. I couldn't find Gilson. So I reckon we need to go back and tell Mr. and Mrs. O'Day. We all need to get back before someone figures out we're gone."

Joslyn peeked over her shoulder. "You mean, you're just going to let him follow you?"

"I don't know how to stop him," Retta replied. "I've reprimanded him quite severely. He seems intent on ignoring my commands."

They trudged through the grass toward the next candle. The wind drifted to their faces, and they shielded the candle flames with their hands.

"Did you find her?" Ben called out.

"No," Retta yelled. "No sign of her anywhere."

"You didn't find anything?" he hollered through the darkness.

Joslyn scurried ahead. "Retta found a buffalo."

"Yeah, sure, and I suppose it ran off."

"No, Retta's buffalo is right here behind us."

"You're joshin' me!"

Joslyn turned and pointed. "Just tell me what that is?"

Ben stared over their shoulders. "Well, I'll be a slop pail at a circus! Look at that! Retta has a buffalo!" he shouted.

The girls tromped past him and kept going.

"That's what we told you," Joslyn said.

Ben hurried to catch up with them. "Why is it following you, Retta?"

"I haven't the slightest notion. But I didn't find any sign of Gilson, and so we're going back."

"And he's goin' with you?" Ben asked.

"Apparently. At least for a while."

They hiked another two hundred feet up the slope.

"Ansley, guess what?" Ben yelled.

The red-headed girl stood on her tiptoes as if it would help her see in the dark. "You found Gilson?"

Ben continued to sprint up the hill. "No. But Retta's got herself a buffalo."

Ansley wrinkled her nose. "What do you mean, she's got a buffalo? Is that some frontier expression like 'seeing the elephant'?"

"Look!" Ben shouted. "It's a real on-the-hoof buffalo!"

"Oh!" Ansley gasped. "Oh!" The candle tumbled from her hand, and immediately thick weeds began to blaze.

Ben, Retta, and Joslyn ran over and stomped on the flames. Within a minute, the fire was reduced to smoke.

Ansley stood frozen in place. "Sorry. I've never seen a buffalo . . . this close . . . in the night. . . . He's huge!"

Ben retrieved her candle and relit it from his.

Retta led the gang toward the wagon.

"I'll be more careful. Really," Ansley promised. "I was just startled." She sniffed the air. "What's that funny smell? Does he smell? Eh, why is he limping?"

"He's shot," Joslyn reported.

Ansley looked back at the shadowy bison and then hurried up ahead of them. "You shot him with my gun? I didn't hear any gunfire."

"No, I didn't shoot him," Joslyn said.

Ben tugged his hat down a little lower in the front. "Someone shot him, and he's injured. That's why he can't go very fast."

Ansley's candle blew out. She relit it off of Ben's. "Does he just follow Retta?" she asked.

Retta rubbed her nose with the back of the hand that held the coup stick. "Yes. And I don't know why."

The foursome stopped several times on the ascent to relight candles that blew out. The breeze was light, but cool and steady. The ground was soft under their shoes. Finally they came up on the crest where Travis waited, his candle almost burned down to his fingers.

"What was all the noise?" he called out as they approached.

"Don't ask," Retta replied and kept walking.

Travis fell in step with Ben. "What does she mean, 'don't ask'?"

Ben pointed his thumb over his shoulder. "There's a very large, wounded buffalo following Retta. That's all. And, no, we didn't find any trace of Gilson."

Travis spun around.

"I—I see it, but I don't believe it! It's—it's like a dream," he stammered.

"Yeah," Joslyn said, "but we don't know yet if it's a good dream or a nightmare."

Ben led the procession back toward Christen where the grass got shorter, and the prairie was almost flat. For a while no one spoke.

Retta's gaze was straight ahead. *Lord, now I'm really, really worried about Gilson. I was counting on finding her, but we didn't do a very good job.*

"Maybe Gilson decided to go back to the wagon," Joslyn offered.

"Yeah, maybe she's waiting for us," Ansley said.

"Is he still back there?" Ben whispered.

Travis looked over his shoulder. "Yeah."

"I think Gilson is gone. I really do. She always does what she says she'll do," Retta said.

Christen tromped out to meet them. "You've been gone a long time. What happened? Didn't you find her?"

"We found nothing," Retta said. "Let's go see Mrs. O'Day."

"Retta did find that buffalo," Travis murmured.

"What buffalo?" Christen asked.

"The one that's following her like a lost puppy," Joslyn replied.

Christen held her candle way above her head. "I can't see any buffalo."

"Where did he go, Retta?" Travis asked.

Retta turned around and stared at the black prairie night. "I told him to go away. Maybe he minded me."

"Maybe he smelled the wagon train," Travis suggested. "Them buffalo have good noses, you know."

"I want to see the buffalo," Christen insisted.

"He's gone, I guess. He looked like any other buffalo," Ben said.

Ansley shook her head. Her red hair fell back perfectly into place. "Except he was shot."

"And limped." Joslyn handed the revolver back to Ansley.

"He had sad, tired eyes," Retta commented.

Christen grabbed Retta's arm. "Really?"

Retta let out a deep sigh. "Yeah, sort of like Gilson's eyes lately."

"I want to see him," Christen demanded again.

Travis pointed into the night. "He's back there someplace. Go look for him if you want to."

"By myself? You come with me, Ben."

He pushed his hat back, revealing tufts of curly blond hair. "Me? Why me?"

"Because you're my brother."

"Oh, come on. We'll all look," Retta directed. "But we won't go very far."

"I'll stay here as a sentinel," Ansley offered. "I've already seen all of him I want to. He stinks."

"Everybody spread out a few feet and walk until Ansley's candle looks dim. Then we'll come back," Retta instructed. "I'll go over here to the left."

"I'm goin' with Retta," Christen announced.

Joslyn giggled. "And I'll go with Travis and Ben."

"We're looking for that buffalo, remember?" Retta hollered.

"Yes, Mama!"

Retta and Christen had hiked thirty or forty yards when they came up to a clump of prairie grass several feet taller than the rest.

"Hold my candle. Let me peek in here." Retta parted

the grass to find the huge buffalo's head inches from hers. His eyes were closed.

"Ohhhhh!" Christen screamed. "It *is* a buffalo!"

Retta flinched.

The buffalo didn't.

"Hey, everyone, he's over here," Christen called out. "Retta found him."

"Give me my candle," Retta said. "Maybe there's another buffalo. . . . There's something down here."

She squatted down next to the buffalo and held out her candle. "Gilson! It's Gilson!"

"Is she . . ." Christen gasped. "I'm going to faint."

"She's breathing. I think she's just exhausted and asleep."

Travis, Ben, and Joslyn ran toward them.

"I've got to get her up," Retta mumbled.

With brush on one side and the buffalo on the other, she couldn't kneel down at Gilson's side.

"You've really got to move," she commanded the buffalo. "I know you don't feel well, but we have to get Gilson up."

She poked the buffalo with the coup stick.

He didn't move.

Gilson opened her eyes. Her weak voice was barely audible. "Retta? Oh, Retta." She started to cry. "I knew you'd come look for me. I just knew it."

"Gilson, let me move this beast. Then I'll help you up." She turned to the animal. "This is really intolerable, Mr. Buffalo. I insist that you move right this minute!"

Just as the others arrived and held up their candles, Retta shoved her shoulder against the sitting buffalo. She jammed her hand into his enormous head, and the coup stick, which was strapped to her wrist, whipped around and bonked the buffalo on the nose.

Suddenly, like a tree felled in the forest, the huge animal toppled over with a thud, his legs sticking out in front of him.

"Did you see that?" Travis gasped. "Retta killed a buffalo with her coup stick!"

"No, I think the poor thing sat down and died before I got here. I merely shoved him over. Ben, help me get Gilson up."

Gilson's voice was weak and raspy. "Retta, I don't want to die."

"I know, Gilson. I know. Let's get you back to your mama."

Ansley MacGregor sprinted through the grass, shielding her candle with her hand. "What happened? What did I miss?"

"Retta done killed that buffalo with her coup stick and saved Gilson's life," Travis shouted.

For a list of other books
by this author
write:
Stephen Bly
Winchester, Idaho 83555
or check out his website:
www.blybooks.com